ERLE STANLEY GARDNER

- Cited by the *Guinness Book of World Records* as the #1 bestselling writer of all time!

- Author of more than 150 clever, authentic, and sophisticated mystery novels!

- Creator of the amazing Perry Mason, the savvy Della Street, and dynamite detective Paul Drake!

- THE ONLY AUTHOR WHO OUTSELLS AGATHA CHRISTIE, HAROLD ROBBINS, BARBARA CARTLAND, AND LOUIS L'AMOUR *COMBINED*!

Why?
Because he writes the best, most fascinating whodunits of all!

You'll want to read every one of them,
from
BALLANTINE BOOKS

D0819478

Also by Erle Stanley Gardner
Published by Ballantine Books:

The Case of the
Fan-Dancer's Horse

Erle Stanley Gardner

BALLANTINE BOOKS · NEW YORK

Copyright © 1947 by Erle Stanley Gardner
Copyright renewed 1975 by Jean Bethell Gardner and Grace Naso

All rights reserved under International and Pan-American Copyright Conventions. Published in the United States of America by Ballantine Books, a division of Random House, Inc., New York, and simultaneously in Canada by Random House of Canada Limited, Toronto.

ISBN 0–345–37144–5

This edition published by arrangement with William Morrow and Company, Inc.

Printed in Canada

First Ballantine Books Edition: October 1992

Chapter 1

It was a blistering hot morning in the Imperial Valley.

The big sedan speeding up behind the car Perry Mason was driving rocketed past at eighty miles an hour, the air currents generated by its passing swayed the lawyer's car on its springs.

"How do you suppose his tyres stand up?" Mason asked Della Street, his secretary. "They must be melting."

Della Street leaned forward in the seat, so that the hot dry air could circulate around her shoulders, evaporating the perspiration. "Perhaps he hasn't gone far . . . Oh! He's going to hit that car!"

Mason instinctively slammed on his own brakes as he saw the car ahead weave slightly as it swung to the left to pass another car going in the same direction. An oncoming car caused the driver of the big sedan to cut in. Fenders seemed only to have given a gentle kiss, but the northbound car went out of control, teetered on two wheels, swerved off the highway into the hot sand, and rolled over.

A cloud of dust which obstructed what was taking place was still hanging over the scene as Mason eased his car to a stop and jumped out.

The overturned car was a jalopy of ancient vintage, all but devoid of paint, its old-fashioned, high wheels making it seem strangely anachronistic. It lay quietly on the desert as though, having wrestled too long with the vicissitudes of life, this crowning misfortune had taken all the fight out of it.

A door on the upper side was slowly pushed open and as Mason approached the vehicle a Mexican woman groped with age-stiffened fingers for sufficient support to enable her to get out of the machine.

Mason helped her out of the car, noticing as he did so that

1

one arm was dangling uselessly. It brushed against the edge of the door and she winced sharply with pain.

But her voice was calm with the courtesy of the polite race. She said, *"Gracias, Señor."*

"Are you hurt anywhere except the broken arm?" Mason asked.

The old Mexican woman's face, lined with the placidity of one who has learned to take life as it comes, regarded him calmly. "No speek Ingleesh," she said.

The driver of another car, who had stopped out of curiosity, said, "Perhaps I can help. I was raised on the border. I speak it like a native. My name's Newell. A big sedan went past me eighty miles an hour. I suppose it's responsible for this."

"Yes. I'm trying to find out whether she's hurt."

Newell engaged in a somewhat one-sided conversation in Spanish, then reported to Mason, "She says that only her arm is hurt. That, she thinks, is broken."

"We'd better get her to a doctor," Mason said. "What's her name?"

"Maria Gonzales."

"Where does she live?"

"She says, 'With her nephew.' "

"Where?"

The woman waved her good arm in an inclusive gesture.

"Here in the Valley," Newell reported.

Mason smiled. "That's rather vague. Let's have a look at her driving licence."

"I'm afraid you're not going to get very far with this," Newell said. "They have a way of quitting cold on you, just going around in circles. Very nice and courteous, but just going round and round."

"But why doesn't she want us to know where she lives?"

"Oh, it probably isn't that. It's the fact that she just doesn't react well to questions, or she may think you're going to make trouble for someone. Just a minute, I'll find out about the driving licence."

He questioned her in Spanish and smiled as he translated the reply. "She says, 'But I am not driving the car.' "

"But she *was* driving the car," Mason said.

Newell interpreted. The old woman indicated the car lying on its side, and something in Spanish which Newell translated. "It is not on the highway. It cannot move. There is no one in it. Therefore no licence is required."

"She must have a driving licence," Mason said.

Newell grinned. "She says, 'But with one arm, Señor, I cannot drive.' "

"Oh, well," Mason said, "there's a registration certificate on the automobile. Not that it makes any difference. Where's the nearest hospital?"

Another northbound car had stopped and a wooden-faced Mexican some forty-five years of age approached them. "Someone is hurt?" he inquired courteously.

"This woman," Mason said. "She was driving the car. She has a broken arm, I believe."

The Mexican looked at the car, then at the woman. He asked four or five rapid-fire questions and received equally rapid answers. "I will take her to a doctor," he said.

"Do you know her?"

"I know her relatives."

Mason started to hand the man one of his business cards, then fearful that the words "attorney at law" on the card would be taken as an ambulance-chasing solicitation, took out his notebook and scrawled his name and the address of the apartment house where he lived.

"In case she should want a witness, my name is Mason. This is Miss Street. We saw the accident. My address is on this paper. Miss Street can be reached through me."

The Mexican gravely inclined his head. "Many thanks. My own name is José Campo Colima, and now, if you will pardon me, I will assist this unfortunate woman."

With courtly grace the Mexican escorted the injured woman to his automobile and tenderly placed her inside. A door slammed and the car was off down the hot highway.

"Well," Newell said, "I'll be on my way. Here's my card. We'd better see that she gets something out of that chap."

"If we can ever find the driver of that other car," Mason said.

"I'll drive in to Calexico and telephone the highway police."

3

"See what you can do," Mason said.

He started back to his own car as Newell drove away, then said, suddenly, "I wonder if that woman left anything in her car, Della? She might have some personal belongings in there which she forgot about in the excitement. We'd better take a look just to be sure. I'd hate to leave any of her property in the car."

Already, the sun, beating down on the exposed metal of the car, made it almost too hot to touch with the bare hand. The door, however, was still open and Mason peered inside.

The upholstery was battered and tattered. There was an aura of dispirited obsolescence about the entire interior, but it was void of any sign of personal belongings.

Mason looked for the registration certificate on the post of the steering wheel. There was none.

"Well," the lawyer said, "we'd better take a look in the trunk just to make certain."

Mason pulled up the cover, then regarded the contents with some surprise.

"What is it?" Della asked.

"Apparently two very fine ostrich-plume fans initialled L.F.," he said, "and that seems to be about all. No, wait a minute. Here's a pair of white dancing slippers. The trunk's recently been lined with clean newspapers. It looks like we're standing in the middle of a fan-dancer's wardrobe."

"I'll bet that's exactly what it is!" Della Street exclaimed. "How in the world would it get in this sort of a car?"

"There's probably a local night club around here. Perhaps her granddaughter is an entertainer. Those newspapers look clean. They must have been freshly pasted in the trunk. What's the date, Della?"

"They're Los Angeles newspapers," she said. "Yesterday's papers."

"Well, we'd better take the fans along. We'll call the police later on and get the woman's address from the accident report. Let's get out of this oven, Della. I'm so dehydrated now that all I need is a cellophane wrapper and a label to be desiccated soup."

Chapter 2

It was in his office the next day that Della Street reminded Perry Mason of the auto accident. As she handed him a sheaf of letters, she said, "That automobile accident, Chief. You telephoned the police at El Centro last night. They were going to notify you."

Mason said, "Get them on the phone, Della. We can't have fan-dancers running around naked."

Della Street laughed, put the call through, and nodded to Mason when his party was on the line.

Mason picked up the receiver, said, "Hello. This is Perry Mason. I left a memo there yesterday about being called in connection with an automobile accident. I have some property which was taken from the car that was crowded off the road. There was a woman with a broken arm. You were going to get her address and call me back."

"Oh, yes," the man said. "I have the memo on my desk, but I didn't call you back because there's been no report of an accident."

"No report made by anyone?"

"No."

"That's strange. The accident took place two or three miles north of Calexico."

"There's a car overturned by the side of the road down there. We investigated and found out the car belonged to a Ramon Calles, who lives in Calexico. He says the car was stolen a couple of days ago."

"Did he report it to the police at the time?" Mason asked.

"No, there's no record of it. He doesn't seem particularly interested. There'll be a repair bill on the car and the cost of towing it to a garage. Calles doesn't seem to think the car is worth that much. You know how these people are. It's pretty hard to get anything out of them when they want to be evasive. They just go around in circles with you in the centre. You can't ever get any nearer to what you're trying to find out. Of course, there's nothing much we can do about it. Were you a witness to the accident?''

"I saw it," Mason said. "A big sedan sideswiped the car and sent it off the road out of control. An old woman was driving this jalopy. Apparently she talked very little English, if any. I would say she was around sixty-five to seventy, with white hair and a rather lined face.''

"You can't tell much about these people. Did she give her name?''

"Maria Gonzales.''

"Could you identify her if you saw her again?''

"Certainly.''

"Of course," the man at the other end of the line said, resignedly, "if we get her and you identify her, then Calles will change his mind about the car being stolen. The driver will turn out to be his grandmother, or his Aunt Mary, or someone and she took the car without telling him about it and it's all right and that'll be that. However, we'll look into it.''

"My interest," Mason said, "is in returning some property that was in the back of the car.''

"Okay, we'll let you know. And you might put an ad in the local paper—about the property.''

Mason hung up, said to Della Street, "Know anything about fan-dancing, Della?''

"Were you suggesting I take up the profession?''

"Why not?" Mason asked. "We seem to have been left with a complete wardrobe.''

"No information down there?''

"Not a scrap. The car that was crowded off the highway is supposed to have been stolen. I don't know who would want to steal a car like that. Ring up the newspaper down in the Valley, Della, and put an ad in the lost-and-found. Make it in general terms. *'If the fan-dancer who has lost certain property will communicate with box so-and-so, she can have*

6

her property restored to her.' Then have the newspaper forward any replies to the office here. Okay, let's look at that mail.''

o mano y aunaha Oper. Then, into the new game we want any nemount the sitter. It lor, Chow the skot of in that

Chapter 3

On Monday morning, Mason, entering his office with springy step, scaled his hat in the general direction of the hat shelf in the coat closet, grinned at Della Street, and said, "The time approaches, Della, for fall vacations, for big-game hunting, for pack trips in the high rugged mountains, sleeping out in the open under the stars, watching the pine trees silhouetted against the star-studded heavens, then awakening to the crisp grey dawn with the wrangler chopping wood for the fire. A moment later the trees glow with the reflection of flames, you hear the crackling of burning wood, and shortly after that you smell the aroma of coffee, and . . ."

"And shortly after that," Della Street interrupted firmly, "one comes down to earth and this stack of unanswered mail."

"Della, don't tell me you're going to pour business responsibilities on my defenceless shoulders. I hate letters."

"You forget about your girl friend."

"My girl friend?"

"The fan-dancer."

Mason's face lit up. "Ah, yes, the Cinderella of the Fans. Last week it seemed important, now it seems slightly absurd. Picture a prominent member of the bar, Della, running up and down through the heat of the Imperial Valley holding a pair of ostrich-plume fans in his left hand, slippers—dainty dancing slippers—in his right hand, a modern Cinderella story. Diogenes with his lantern is an old stodgy compared to the lawyer looking for his fan-dancing Cinderella. And how do you suppose she will be dressed when I find her, inasmuch as I will be holding her wardrobe in my left hand? The thought is intriguing, Della. It has possibilities."

8

"It has more than possibilities," Della Street said. "We have an answer to your ad."

"Aha! so we've located the fan-dancer that lost the fans?"

"Not the fans," Della said.

"Not the fans?" Mason echoed.

"No, the horse."

Mason looked at her quizzically. "Are you perhaps trying a little ribbing?"

Della Street handed him an envelope addressed to a newspaper box. Mason shook out a folded sheet of notepaper.

"Smell it," Della said.

Mason sniffed at the heavy scent and grinned. "Woof! Woof! I'm a wolf, Della!"

He unfolded the paper. To the top of the sheet had been clipped the ad taken from the newspaper. Below the ad in rather distinctive feminine handwriting had been penned the message. Mason read it aloud.

"The salutation," he said, "starts chastely enough. 'Dear Box 9062,' and then right away the letter plunges into passion. 'Oh you darling! It was so sweet of you to go to the trouble of putting the ad in the paper. I've been so worried about him. A girl in my occupation follows pretty much a regular circuit; for instance, I was a week in Brawley and then went on to this town. Then I'll play four or five night spots in the central part of the state. Fan-dancing isn't what it used to be. We were pushed out of most of the city spots by the strip tease, and now even that's on its way out, but in the country places, which like to be sophisticated, a *good* fan-dancer can get by.' "

Mason looked up from the letter and said, "The word 'good' is underscored. I suppose you noticed that, Della?"

"Yes, I wondered just what that meant," Della Street said archly.

Mason laughed. His face showing his enjoyment, he went on reading. " 'I am very much attached to my horse. When he broke out of the place where I had him pastured in Brawley, and got away, I was heartbroken. I made inquiries, but simply couldn't find out a thing. However, the man who rented me the pasture told me it was almost certain the horse

9

would be recovered because down in that country people are very careful about returning stray stock, and there's very little natural pasturage.' "

" 'I'll have my agent get in touch with you through the newspaper and see that you are suitably reimbursed, and will you please deliver the horse to the party who has my written order. You can check the handwriting to make certain you have the right party. And thank you all over again. Sincerely yours.' "

Mason went on quizzically, "And the epistle is signed Lois Fenton with the parenthetical statement. 'Whose stage name is "Cherie Chi-Chi." ' "

The door from the reception room opened. Gertie, the telephone operator and receptionist, said, "Excuse the interruption, Mr. Mason. I wasn't certain I had it right, so I thought I'd better ask you about it. There's a man in the office who wants to see you about a horse."

"His name?" Mason asked.

"He says his name is John Callender, and that you won't know him personally, but that he is the agent of Lois Fenton."

Mason grinned. "The fan-dancer's boy friend! What does he look like, Gertie—a stage-door Johnnie?"

"Not at all. He's got a strong face, is well-tailored and sort of . . . well, a big shot."

"Probably an angel," Mason said. "Does he act a little self-conscious or embarrassed?"

"Not that I could see."

Mason drummed with his finger tips on the edge of his desk. "You'd think he would, Gertie. A man of some affluence, running around to a lawyer's office doing a fan-dancer's errands. Let's have a look at him, Gertie. Send him in."

"Yes, sir, I didn't know. When he said he was—well, you know, about a horse."

When Gertie had left the office, Della Street asked, somewhat apprehensively, "Are you going to tell him it's all a mistake, Chief?"

"I don't think so. We'll let him do the talking. The thing

interests me. After all, we find a couple of fans and a pair of dancing slippers and then . . ."

The door opened and Gertie announced, "Mr. John Callender."

Callender's face was twisted into a most cordial smile. It seemed assumed, however, as though he had forced stiff facial muscles into an unaccustomed mask.

"Mr. Mason, this *is* a pleasure!"

Mason shook hands, said, "Sit down. This is my secretary, Miss Street. What is it you want?"

Callender settled himself in the big, overstuffed client's chair. He had about himself an air of complete assurance, the manner of one who is accustomed to command and who finds himself in an unusual position when called upon to ask for favours.

"I am the agent of Lois Fenton, sometimes known as 'Cherie Chi-Chi,' " he said, and smiled with effusive cordiality.

"Indeed," Mason observed.

"I called about the horse."

"And what about the horse?"

"I want it."

"May I ask how you happened to discover my identity? After all, I put an ad in the local paper using only a box number."

"Come, come, Mr. Mason. Surely in a matter of this importance you didn't expect Miss Fenton to deal only with a box number."

"Nevertheless, I would be interested to ascertain how she discovered my real identity."

"Quite simple, Mr. Mason, quite simple."

"Would you mind telling me the exact technique?"

"I confess I was forced to resort to subterfuge."

"And what was the subterfuge?"

Callender shifted his position. The smile was gone from his face now, leaving steel-cold eyes, and a thin mouth as straight and grim as though it were a piece of taut string.

"Specifically, Mr. Mason, I desired very much to learn the identity of the person with whom I had to deal. I advised

11

the newspaper that the party who had placed the ad wished to have it run for another week, that I would pay for it and I requested a receipt. I paid in cash and was given a receipt in the name of Mr. Perry Mason, with your office address, and the box number used in the ad duly noted on the receipt."

"Rather simple, wasn't it?" Mason said.

"After all, Mr. Mason, this is a surprise. We expected to be dealing with some rancher in the Imperial Valley, who would perhaps be indignant because of a broken fence and trampled crops. We were prepared to be most generous in a financial way. I presume, of course, that means nothing to you?"

"Less than nothing."

"But," Callender went on, hurriedly, "in view of the fact that your time is so valuable, Mr. Mason, and you have been called upon to extend it in connection with the affairs of my er . . . er . . . I suppose we might say client, I am . . ."

"Are you a lawyer?" Mason asked.

"Heaven forbid! No, no—now don't take any offence—I didn't mean it exactly that way. I merely meant that the life of a lawyer would hardly appeal to me. I am a rancher, Mr. Mason. I have a fairly large estate in the Imperial Valley, between Calexico and El Centro, a very nice place. I do a little horse-breeding and am very much interested in horses."

Mason said, "You have something with you to prove your identity, Mr. Callender?"

For a moment Callender's face darkened angrily, then he said, "Why certainly, Mr. Mason." He produced a billfold and extracted a driver's licence, a membership card in a country club, and a card showing membership in the Automobile Club of Southern California.

"Thank you," Mason said. "Now, can you describe the property?"

"Yes, indeed, Mr. Mason. He's a chestnut gelding, fifteen hands high, with one white hind foot—the right. There's a white star on the forehead. The horse is seven years old, perfectly sound, American saddle-bred."

Mason said, "I'm sorry. I can't help you."

"You mean you refuse to turn over that horse?"

"I mean that I can't help you."

"Look here, Mason, I don't think you know with whom you're dealing. Perhaps you'd better investigate. You'll find that I'm not a man to be trifled with. I . . ."

"But," Mason interrupted, "you have not described the property."

"Not described it!" Callender said. "You're crazy! I raised that horse. Why . . ."

"You still haven't described the property accurately enough for me to turn it over."

"Good heavens, what more do you want? The horse has a very slight scar on the inside of the left front leg. It has an unusually long tail . . ."

Callender suddenly smiled again. "Oh, yes," he said. "You'll pardon me. I forgot the first thing I was supposed to do."

He opened his pocket, took out a sheet of paper and handed it to Mason.

The sheet bore the same heavy scent as that of the letter Mason had received, and read:

Dear Box 9062: The enclosed will introduce Mr. John Callender, who is hereby authorized to receive from the finder the horse which I lost a few days ago, said horse being described as American saddle-bred, gelding, fifteen hands high, white star on forehead, white right hind foot. Mr. Callender will accept delivery on my behalf and for me will pay any and all claims and incidental expenses.

LOIS FENTON
(Stage Name "Cherie Chi-Chi")

"The property which I found," Mason said, "does not exactly answer that description."

"Well, tell me where it differs," Callender challenged.

Mason smiled and shook his head. "In dealing with lost property it's up to the claimant to describe it perfectly."

"Perhaps some little thing, some little minor thing that's happened since I last saw the horse, a wire scratch or something of that sort, something that doesn't affect the basic

13

description of the horse in the least. If it's a matter of money, I'll be glad to . . ."

"It isn't a matter of money."

"What is it, then?"

"I want you to describe the property."

Callender took a deep breath. "Look here, Mr. Mason, I'll meet your own terms, whatever they may be. Just name the figure. Here, I'll write you a cheque for five hundred dollars. That will cover your expenses in the matter and the amount of time you've had to expend. I probably should have made that approach first."

Mason said, "I told you it wasn't a question of money, Mr. Callender."

Callender got up out of his chair. "I suppose you've sold me out somewhere along the line. I don't think you can get away with this. Damn it, Mason, I know some law. I'll have you arrested for extortion."

"Just what have I tried to extort?"

"You're trying to hold me up."

"I told you," Mason said, "it wasn't a question of money."

"The devil it isn't! You're just sitting back there, waiting for me to boost my offer. I won't do it. I'm staying at the Richmell Hotel. I'll give you until five o'clock this evening to surrender that horse. At the end of that time I'll take steps. And five hundred dollars is my limit. Good day."

Callender turned back toward the door through which he had entered, then, seeing the exit door, veered sharply to the left. Only the door check prevented him from slamming the door shut.

Suddenly he caught himself, turned and pushed his way back through the closing door. He was all affability once more. "Of course," he said, returning to bend over Mason's desk, "I know what's wrong. I didn't describe the property accurately."

"Go ahead," Mason invited.

Callender lowered his head to a level with Mason's ear and said in a whisper, "The bullet wound."

"Where?" Mason whispered.

14

"On the horse," Callender said, smiling.

Mason shook his head.

Callender straightened, frowned, started to say something else, changed his mind and stalked out of the office.

Mason cocked a quizzical eyebrow at Della Street.

She said, "That seems to be a horse on Mr. Callender."

"Or a horse on us," Mason observed thoughtfully. "I'm afraid we're going to investigate, Della. That crack about the bullet . . ."

The telephone on Della Street's desk rang sharply. Della Street picked it up, said, "All right, Gertie, what is it. . . ? Just a moment."

She turned to Perry Mason. "Another man out there," she said, "wanting to see you about a horse."

"What's *his* name?"

"Arthur Sheldon."

"Let's see what Mr. Sheldon has to say, Della. Tell Gertie to send him right in. One would think we were running a livery stable."

Arthur Sheldon was in his late twenties, a brown-eyed, light-haired man with quick, nervous mannerisms and a rapid-fire manner of speaking.

"Good morning, Mr. Mason. It was nice of you to see me. My name's Sheldon, Arthur Sheldon. I can tell you what I want in a very few words. John Callender has just been in here. What did he want? What did he say?"

Mason smiled. "Even if I knew your interest in the matter and it proved to be legitimate, I could hardly divulge the information you have requested."

"Oh, I'm sorry," Sheldon blurted, flushing. "I hadn't realized just exactly how that was going to sound. Look here, Mr. Mason, you aren't going to give him the horse, are you?"

"No," Mason said, and then added, "not as yet."

"Don't do it. *Please* don't do it. He doesn't own that horse. He gave it to Lois. Look here, Mr. Mason, you're not his lawyer, are you?"

"No."

Sheldon's face showed relief. "That's fine. I want you to represent us."

15

"Us?"

"Well, Lois."

"In what?"

"Well—in case he starts anything."

Mason said, "Now let's get this straight. If you expect to try and bribe me to deliver any certain property to any particular person under the guise of retaining me . . ."

"No, no, it's not that at all. Just so you don't give *him* the horse."

"And what do you want?"

"I want you to represent Lois."

"In what?"

"I've explained to you generally. I want you to see that . . . Look here, Mr. Mason, would you talk with Lois?"

"Why certainly. Can she come here?"

"Not before tomorrow. She's working in a night spot up in Palomino. That's a little town up in the Walker Basin country up back of Bakersfield. She has to be on there tonight, and she wouldn't have time to drive in and get back, but she could come down tomorrow, if you could give her an appointment."

"At what time?" Mason asked.

"Any time after . . . well, let us say after ten o'clock. Any time between ten and two."

"Ten-thirty?" Mason asked.

"I'll have her here," Sheldon promised. "Mr. Mason, I can't begin to tell you how much I appreciate this. You want some money now? I . . ."

"No," Mason said, "not until after I talk with Miss Fenton. How did you happen to get my address?"

"I followed Callender here. I've been following him ever since he got that address from the newspaper. My room in the Richmell Hotel is directly opposite the corridor from his. I have 510. He's in 511."

Mason regarded him with a frown. "I'll know more about your case when I've talked with Lois Fenton. Please see that she keeps her appointment promptly. Ten-thirty on the dot."

When he had gone, Mason said to Della Street, "The

horse with all these claimants, the bullet wound, the fan-dancer. How'd you like to take a drive, Della?"

"Where?"

"To Palomino."

"I'd love it."

"Let's go," Mason said.

Chapter 4

Palomino had originally been a rough western crossroads town. Then overnight, with the advent of heavy construction work on the big dam, the place had mushroomed into a ready-made city.

The old-time buildings, dilapidated and unpainted, had furnished the nucleus for a hastily constructed business district composed of tents, tent-houses, old refrigerator freight cars converted into little storerooms, and occasionally trailers parked broadside to the street, with boards bearing appropriate names tacked along the side.

The Grand Millinery Company did business in a trailer. The Elite Ready-to-Wear was housed in a reconstructed freight car and the Ritz Hotel consisted of an elaborate front behind which were some four or five dozen tent-houses, arranged in rows like army barracks.

The sprawling unpainted building which had been known as Myer's Hall in the days when an occasional mountain dance had been held at the crossroads, now housed a tumultuous night club known as "The Shamrock."

Electricity had become one of the cheapest commodities available and over the strange assortment of human habitations, light blazed in white brilliance. Reconditioned box cars sported glaring red neon signs and on the sides of "The Shamrock" an artist had painted a trifoliate in vivid green, the colour being further enhanced by green lights. These lights invested the place with a weird and bizarre unreality. Men and women moving in and out of the night club assumed for the moment the ghastly appearance of animated corpses.

Inside the place, the floor had been crowded with tables until only a small square remained at one side of the barnlike room, and here a five-piece "orchestra" manufactured music which made up in volume anything it lacked in harmony.

Perry Mason and Della Street, having by virtue of an out-of-town mien secured a table near the orchestra, exchanged snatches of conversation in between numbers of the floor show and the blaring of the music.

"There is," Della Street observed over her coffee, "a rough and ready air about the place that's . . . well, it's like waiting for dynamite to be set off."

"It's rough and it's ready for trouble," Mason said.

A broad-shouldered, ham-fisted man in a coarse suit which hung loosely from the belt, but which was stretched taut across the powerful shoulders, stood over the table grinning.

"Beg your pardon, Mister," he said to Perry Mason, "but we're just a little short of dancing partners up here. I'm a committee from the table over there. A committee of one. We think the young lady had ought to dance."

Della Street flashed him a smile. "Sorry," she said, "I'm not dancing tonight."

"Well, now, that's a shame. We couldn't change your mind?"

Her smile was friendly, but her voice was firm. "Definitely not. I'm sorry."

"So'm I."

The man stood there awkwardly for a moment, then turned and walked back to a table where three other men were sitting. His face reddened somewhat at the raucous laughter of their greeting as he once more sat down.

"I wish she'd come out," Della Street said, "and let us get out of here. You sent her a message, Chief?"

"That's right—through the master of ceremonies. And the five-dollar bill that I used as a postage stamp should have been a guarantee of delivery."

The lights dimmed and the master of ceremonies announced the feature performance of the evening, little Miss Cherie Chi-Chi, the wonderful, incomparable light-footed dancer.

The orchestra made noise. The lights went down until there was almost total darkness, then flared up in a deep green simulation of moonlight. Bare feet thudded on the floor. From the crowded masculine humanity which packed the place came an audible inhalation, and then, whirling around, with plumed fans showing startlingly white against the deep colour of the spotlight, a girl glided into the centre of the floor.

For a moment Cherie Chi-Chi stood poised, smiling, the fans held so as to conceal much of her body. Then the fans began to move. The slender white body glided through a series of dance steps. The light, a deep violet, now showed high, pointed breasts, a slender waist, smooth hips.

As the eyes of the audience accustomed themselves to the semi-darkness, it seemed that the light was getting stronger. The tempo of the orchestra became faster and faster. Then, suddenly, the figure faced the audience. The fans opened for a moment, then were pressed tightly against the body and the girl's smiling face, white gleaming teeth and the waving plumes of the fan caught the light as she backed from the dance floor, then suddenly turned and vanished through the entrance to the dressing rooms.

The flimsy walls of the place threatened to bulge out and collapse with the roar of applause.

The lights went on hurriedly, signifying that there would be no encore.

Della Street glanced at Mason. "Some dance," she said.

"Darn good-looking kid," Mason observed. "Apparently she has no Mexican blood though, very white skin, red hair— the eyes, I believe, were blue."

"Yes, I saw you studying her face."

Mason grinned.

The audience continued to demand an encore, but the master of ceremonies announced two gifted hula dancers straight from the Island of Oahu. Someone started ukulele music and once more the lights went down.

The grass-skirted, full-figured, tawny girls who bounded out into the spotlight soon demonstrated their ability to hold the attention of the masculine audience anywhere.

By the conclusion of the second hula, the two Hawaiians had so completely captivated the audience no one recognized

Cherie Chi-Chi, attired now in a neat-fitting suit of small patterned plaid which made it almost appear to be a tweed, when she glided quietly up to Mason's table.

He was on his feet at once. "Do sit down," he invited.

"Thank you. The head waiter gave me your note."

"I'm Mr. Mason. This is Miss Street, my secretary."

She smiled a greeting to Della, said to Mason, "You're the man who put the ad in the paper in El Centro?"

"Yes."

"Did you see a Mr. Callender?" she asked.

"I saw him."

"Oh," she said, shortly, and made no other comment.

"How about a drink?" Mason asked.

She nodded. A waiter who had been watching her attentively, glided quickly to her side.

"The usual thing, Harry," she said.

The waiter glanced inquiringly at Perry Mason and Della Street.

"We'll nurse these," Mason said.

The waiter noiselessly dissolved into the blue haze of tobacco smoke which hung over the tables.

"Been here long?" Mason asked.

"Not very."

"Like it?"

"Uh huh."

"You seem to know the waiter quite well."

She laughed and said, "We all of us pull together. Something about a job like this that makes you get acquainted fast and stay friendly." Her eyes became wistful as she went on. "Travelling around this way, those who are in the same line of work are the only friends you have. The real friends."

"What's the elevation up here?" Mason asked.

"Around fifty-five hundred. We're a little over a mile high."

"Quite a change in the climate from the Imperial Valley."

"Yes, isn't it?"

"Well," Mason asked, laughingly, "are you going to ask about your property?"

"My horse?"

21

"Of course," Mason observed, "as the finder of property, I have to keep it in the vague category of personal property until you have identified it."

"But it's mine."

"All you have to do is to identify it."

"A chestnut horse. A little taller than the average. He handles his legs nicely. Slim barrelled, hot-blooded, but not *too* hot. A saddle made by Bill Wyatt, Austin, Texas."

"Anything else?" Mason asked.

"Oh, yes, a Navajo blanket and a quilted under-pad to go next to the horse."

"You have had the horse long?" Mason asked.

"Two or three months."

"White star on the forehead?"

"That's right."

"One white hind foot?"

"Yes, the right."

Mason smiled and said, "I haven't seen him."

She was frowning now, irritably. "Don't be silly."

"I tell you, I haven't seen him."

"Of course you have. You even know the description. You know about that star on the forehead and you know about the white right hind foot."

"Just because I describe a horse doesn't mean I have him."

The waiter brought the drink.

She said, angrily, "What are you trying to do, hold me up? Is this a blackmail proposition?"

The waiter produced a check from his pocket, stood casually by the table.

"Simply put it all on my check," Mason said.

"Yes, sir." The big waiter moved closer to the table. "The drink all right, Miss Cherie?" he asked.

She smiled at him. "Fine, thanks."

He continued to hover around.

Cherie Chi-Chi looked at Perry Mason. "You didn't find a horse?"

Mason made his smile affable. "No horse."

The index finger of her left hand was tracing little designs on the tablecloth. "You found something. You put an ad in the paper."

Mason nodded. The waiter whisked an imaginary crumb from the corner of the table with a napkin.

"You found something . . ." Suddenly her finger stopped its motion. She raised eyelashes heavy with mascara. "You found two fans," she said. "Two ostrich-plume fans with the initials 'L.F.' on them. You found a pair of high-heeled slippers."

Mason nodded.

She threw back her head and laughed. "And I thought it was the horse! That's all, Harry. The drink's fine. I won't need you anymore."

The waiter abruptly withdrew.

"Where are they?" Cherie Chi-Chi asked.

"In my car."

She laughed. "All right, I'll identify them. They were made by a firm in St. Louis. The initials 'L.F.' are inlaid in the fans in gold and the slippers were also made in St. Louis. I can give you the name of the store, if I think long enough."

"You won't need to. Unquestionably the property is yours. When do you want it?"

"Now."

"Where?"

"Here."

Mason said, "Will you hold the fort, Della? I'll get the package."

He left the girls, threaded his way through the crowded tables, then went out in the cold, crisp mountain air, unlocked his car, took out a small suitcase and was just locking the car again when he was conscious of a figure standing behind him.

Mason moved quickly, yet tried to keep from giving the appearance of whirling.

Harry, the big waiter, said, "She sent me out to get them, sir, so you wouldn't have to bother taking them in."

"It's all right," Mason said. "I'll deliver them to her personally."

"But I can take them right in through the back entrance, if you don't mind."

"I think I'd prefer to give them to her personally. Perhaps I can go in through the back door with you."

"Yes, sir. Very good, sir. Right this way, please."

Mason followed the man around past the parked cars, detoured a row of sour-smelling garbage pails, and went down three steps to a door which the waiter unlocked with a key he took from his pocket. They hurried along a passageway, climbed some stairs, and walked past a row of dressing rooms.

Doors were open. Show girls without any vestige of self-consciousness were in various stages of undress as they changed the scanty garments which were billed as "costumes."

Harry, moving with complete assurance, led the way past the dressing rooms through a little cubby hole where an electrician manipulated the lights, down a short flight of stairs into the kitchen through a service door, and ushered Mason to his table.

Della Street and the fan-dancer were deep in low-voiced conversation.

Cherie Chi-Chi looked up, smiled, "You have them?"

"Yes."

"I told Harry to get them so as to save you carrying them through the crowd. I thought you might feel embarrassed."

"Harry brought me back through the stage door. It wasn't any bother at all. You see I have them in here."

Mason propped the suitcase on his knees, opened the lid.

Cherie Chi-Chi took out one of the fans, opened it, gave a graceful voluptuous sweep as she drew it tantalizingly along the curves of her body. "They're my favourites," she said. "They have a beautiful balance." She handed one of the fans to Della. "Like to try it, honey?"

Della Street took the fan, glanced at Mason, imitated the seductive motions which the fan-dancer had made.

"Oh, oh!" Mason said.

"You do it *won*derfully," Cherie Chi-Chi exclaimed. "Have you ever tried it?"

24

Della smilingly disclaimed any previous practice.

Harry once more hovered over the table. "Everything all right?"

"Everything's all right, Harry, and there'll be no check for this table. It's on me."

"Yes, Miss Cherie."

The heavily made-up eyes regarded Mason intently. "And," she said, "there'll be a reward."

The lights went dim at that moment as a girl who was billed as a nautch dancer, barefooted on to the stage, her feet thudding the boards like the pads of some large wild animal.

Cherie Chi-Chi bent over Mason's chair, her arm circled his neck. "Thank you," she said, and then hot, moist lips were pressed against the lawyer's, held there for a tingling moment and then she was gone.

Della Street laughed at Mason's surprise. "Strawberry?" she asked, as Mason dabbed at the lipstick with his napkin.

"Raspberry," the lawyer said, "and damned thick."

Chapter 5

It was after one o'clock when Mason's car entered the lighted metropolitan district.

"Tired, Della?"

"Not at all. I enjoyed it. It was a beautiful ride. The moonlight on the mountains was like liquid silver."

Mason said, "A beautiful setting for something rather grim, I'm afraid. I'm going to see Arthur Sheldon. I'll take you home first so you can get some rest."

"No, I'd like to stay with it. Why see Arthur Sheldon at this hour in the morning, Chief?"

"I want to find out more about that fan-dancer."

"She was a graceful little thing, wasn't she?"

"Uh huh."

"Why do you suppose it never occurred to her to think about the fans? They were her favourites. She must have known they were lost, and yet, all she could think about was the horse."

"That's one of the things I want to ask Sheldon about."

"He's in the same hotel with Callender?"

"Yes, he has a room directly across the hall, I understand."

"You didn't tell Cherie Chi-Chi anything about him?"

"No."

Della Street said, "That raspberry lipstick seems to have had an effect on your vocal chords. You haven't averaged a word a mile."

"I've been thinking," Mason said. "What's the name of that hotel?"

"The Richmell."

"Know his room number?"

"Five-ten."

26

Mason guided the car silently for a few blocks, then said, "I'll jingle a couple of keys in my hand as we walk across the lobby. Try to make it seem casual, as though we're going up to a room after a show and a midnight supper."

"He'll be in bed."

"We'll get him up."

"You don't want to phone him first?"

"No. The call might attract attention. An operator might listen in and remember about it afterwards. It's late."

"Why so furtive?" she asked.

Mason merely shook his head and smiled.

"Holding out on me?"

"It's not that, Della. I'm just not certain. I want to get a few more facts before I even dare to formulate a theory. . . . Here we are."

Mason had some difficulty finding a parking place near the hotel, even at that hour of the morning. He locked the ignition, said to Della Street, "Remember now, we're a married couple beginning to get just a little bit bored with each other's society. It's been a nice evening and now we're getting back to the humdrum, thinking in terms of tomorrow morning. I'll barge across the lobby a little in advance of you. You can perhaps manage a yawn."

"For heaven's sake," she said, in mock alarm, "is marriage like that?"

Mason said, "it's just an act we're putting on for the benefit of the house dick."

"Do you suppose *he* thinks marriage is like that?"

"I'm quite certain he does. Try walking across a hotel lobby at one-thirty in the morning any other way and you'll find out. Here we go."

They entered the hotel. Mason perfunctorily held the door open for Della Street, started for the elevator when she was still a step behind him, apparently caught himself with a self-conscious gesture, and slowed down to wait impatiently for her to catch up.

They entered the elevator. Mason somewhat tardily removed his hat. "Six," he said.

Della Street glanced swiftly at him, then turned away.

27

The elevator deposited them on the sixth floor. Mason hurried Della Street down the corridor.

"It's 510," she said.

"I know, but I'm trying to protect my clients."

"Who? Lois Fenton?"

"No, us."

Mason opened a door marked STAIRS, ran down the flight of uncarpeted, concrete stairs, pushed open a door at the bottom of the staircase and then suddenly stopped.

"What's the matter?" Della Street whispered.

"Someone coming down the corridor directly toward us," Mason said, letting the door ease back until it held a scant two inches of opening.

"The house detective?"

"No. Hush . . . Della, it's Harry, the big waiter from Palomino."

They stood tense, without motion, holding their breaths, waiting. Through the narrow opening of the door they could hear steps approaching. Then suddenly the steps stopped. Knuckles rapped gently on a door.

They heard a bolt click back. A door opened. A man's voice said, "Hello. You made a quick trip, come in."

The voice of the visitor muttered something that was unintelligible. The room door closed and Mason, waiting a full second, pushed open the door from the staircase and said to Della, "Come on."

"Was that Harry? Are you certain?"

"Yes, that was Harry. I think he went into a room on the other side of the corridor. Let's see. Yes, it's across the corridor from our side. The even numbers are on this side and the odd numbers over there. Wait a minute, Della. That may have been the room, directly across. 511. That's where Callender is supposed to be located."

"Think he's likely to come out?" Della whispered.

"I don't know. We'll have to knock gently on Sheldon's door," Mason said, tapping very lightly with the tips of his fingers. He waited several seconds as nothing happened, then knocked again more loudly.

"Who is it?" a man's voice asked.

28

Mason made no answer. Unshod steps sounded behind the door. The man's voice was closer to the door this time. There was a trace of fear in the voice which came through the panels. "Who is it? I won't open until I know who it is."

Mason took a card from his pocket, slipped it through the crack under the door.

A light switch clicked on in the room. A knife edge of light became visible under the door. Hands on the inside pulled Mason's card the rest of the way through the crack and into the room. There was an interval of silence during which Mason glanced over his shoulder at the door of room number 511. A ribbon of light also was visible beneath the door of that room.

Abruptly there was the sound of a turning bolt, a clicking night latch. The door of 510 opened. Sheldon, standing in bare feet and pyjamas in the doorway, saw Della Street and instinctively ducked back behind the door, trying to close it.

Mason pushed the door open, entered the room, kicked it shut behind him, said, "Sorry, Sheldon, there's no time for being polite."

"I didn't know. Your secretary—you'll pardon me, I'm . . ."

Mason said, "Forget it. Keep your voice low. Come over here. Sit down on the bed. Let's talk things out. You got a robe?"

"Yes."

"Put it on."

"Can I comb my hair, or . . ."

"No."

Sheldon put on a bathrobe, sat down beside Mason and Della Street on the bed.

Mason said, "I saw a fan-dancer. I want to know something more about her."

"What about her?"

Mason said, "I think there's been a ringer."

"What do you mean?"

"I mean a ringer."

"You mean the one in Palomino isn't the right one?"

"Yes."

29

Sheldon sat motionless for several seconds, then he said, "Yes, I guess so. How did you find out?"

"I went up there."

"But you don't know the real Lois."

"I know the ringer."

"I didn't think you'd find out—so soon. What do you want?"

"I want you to come clean. I want you to start talking, and I want you to start talking fast."

"What do you want to know?"

"Who's Cherie Chi-Chi? Who's John Callender? Why is the horse so damn important?"

Sheldon said, "John Callender is . . . that is, in a sense . . ."

"Come on," said Mason, "out with it."

"He's her husband," Sheldon blurted. "The real one. I mean the real Lois."

"And what about the horse?"

"Callender thinks he could use the horse as evidence— that is, if he can find the horse."

Mason said, "If you start at the beginning and give me the whole story we won't waste so much time."

Sheldon said, "It's hard to tell you about Lois Fenton so you'll understand her."

"Then skip her," Mason said, "and just tell me about facts."

Sheldon said, "The facts won't mean anything to you unless you understand Lois."

"Well, Lois won't mean anything to me unless I have the facts."

Sheldon ran his spread fingers through his tousled hair. "The trouble is, there just aren't words to describe that sort of thing. Have you ever seen a deer when it didn't know you were watching it? It's something about the way it walks . . . well, wild is the only way you can express it. Well, that's Lois. She has that same sort of thing about her. She's wild in a sense that she's untamed and just the way she wants to be. You couldn't ever put her into a routine job anywhere."

"And she married Callender?"

"I'm coming to that. There are lots of these carnival girls who are tough. They let the life coarsen them."

"And Lois didn't?" Mason asked. "Is that what you're trying to tell me."

"Exactly. Lois never had any advantages. She wanted to express herself in motion. Look here, Mr. Mason, you say you saw *a* fan-dancer. If you ever saw Lois Fenton, the real Lois Fenton, you wouldn't call her *a* fan-dancer. You don't think of sex when she's dancing, not in that way. You think of beauty."

Mason glanced at Della Street.

Della said, "You're in love with her, perhaps that's why."

Sheldon said, "No, it isn't that. You've got the cart before the horse. It's because she's so beautiful and all of that that I'm in love with her, not that I just think she's beautiful and clean and fine because I'm crazy about her."

Mason said, "All right. Now let's have the facts."

"There are two dancers using the name of Lois Fenton, but the real Lois . . . I can't explain fully right now, Mr. Mason."

Mason said, "I can't do a thing until you've given me the facts and I know where to start working and how to start working."

"Lois Fenton has a brother, Jasper Fenton," Sheldon said. "He's made a lot of trouble for Lois. Callender met Lois. He fell for her like a ton of bricks. Because he was rich, he thought that was all there was to it. Then he found Lois wasn't for lease and wasn't for sale. He gave Jasper a job, running his office. It was a nice job. It had a good salary.

"That's Callender's way. It was easy for Jasper to play the horses. Callender made it easy. He's a deep one, make no mistake about that, Mr. Mason.

"The boy forged two cheques for around three thousand dollars. That gave Callender everything he wanted. Don't try to tell me those crude methods don't work any longer. They do. I saw them work. John Callender is a big shot in his home county. When he whistles, the prosecutor jumps through hoops. Callender pretended that he was surprised and shocked to death. He made it stick. Actually, he'd

31

watched the kid like a hawk, putting temptation in his way and waiting for him to fall. He wanted to make certain the kid stole enough to make restitution impossible, not enough to really hurt. When he gave Jasper that job . . .''

"All right, never mind that," Mason interrupted. "Regardless of whether it should have worked or not, the fact is it *did* work. She married him. Is that right?"

"She married him."

"And broke your heart?" Della Street asked.

"Yes."

"Can you tell us about the marriage?" Della asked.

"Callender trapped her into marriage and it was like trapping a wild thing. Lois was like a wild animal in a cage. But she played fair with John. She would have continued to stay with him until it killed her if he'd played fair with her.

"But he didn't, and Lois pulled out.

"She'd become very much attached to this horse that John had given her. Well, she pulled out and took the horse with her, and then Callender went nuts. He dragged out these old cheques, swore he was going to prosecute Jasper for forgery. Lois claimed her marriage had wiped out that indebtedness; that all she had agreed to do was marry John and give him a chance, fair and square, to prove that the thing would work. Well, a week or so ago someone on horseback quietly rode up to Callender's place, slipped in the office, opened the safe, and was discovered. He got away, but the watchman took a shot at him. He says he knows he hit the horse from the way the animal jumped."

"Why did the burglar ride in on horseback?" Mason asked.

"Because a man on foot would have stood no chance of sneaking into the grounds without having the dogs corner him. But a man on horseback, if he was bold enough and daring enough, and in particular if he had a horse that the dogs knew, could get away with it hands down.

"There's the story in a nutshell, Mr. Mason. The cheque business is pretty well washed up. A jury might not convict when the full story came out. But if Callender can prove that either Lois Fenton or her brother rode her horse up to his house, opened the safe and tried to steal those cheques, he'd then have a brand new hold on her. Callender wants to find Lois' horse. He can't. Lois says someone stole it the night of the burglary—or else that it just strayed away, saddle and all.

"So you can see what happened when your ad appeared in the paper . . . Now then, that's all I know about it."

Mason jerked his thumb toward the door leading into the corridor and said, "And Callender has the room right across the hall."

"That's right."

"You're here trying to spy on him?"

"I want to try to find out what he's doing."

"Does he know you by sight?"

"No."

"By name?"

"I hope not, but he may. I'm not certain about that."

"Just what do you expect to accomplish by keeping an eye on him this way?"

"I don't know. I do know that if he finds that horse and tries to drag Lois back to him that I'll . . . Well, I guess there's nothing I *can* do."

Mason said, impatiently, "Don't lie to me. You're not just spying on him. You intend to search his room when he's out. Is that it?"

Sheldon squirmed uncomfortably inside his robe.

"Is it?" Mason asked.

"Yes."

"You've been in there already?"

"Yes."

"More than once."

"Yes."

"Find anything?"

"Not the cheques. I found a receipt from the newspaper for the want ad. It had your name on it. That's how I knew what Callender wanted when he came to your office."

"You have a key to his room?"

"A pass-key. I borrowed the maid's pass-key for a minute, made a wax impression, had one made."

"And you want me to help Lois Fenton?" Mason asked.

"God, yes. I'll mortgage my soul to pay you. I'll . . ."

"Get out of here," Mason said. "Pack up, check out and beat it. Bring Lois Fenton to my office tomorrow—the real one. Have her there at ten-thirty. Now dress, pack and get out."

"But hotel rooms are scarce, and . . ."

"I said check out."

"I'd have to sleep on a bench in the park or a railroad station . . ."

"I don't give a damn where you sleep. If I'm going to have anything to do with you, I want you to quit being across the hall from this woman's husband. You're crazy about his wife. You dog his steps, shadow his room . . . Get the hell out of this hotel. Leave Callender to me."

Mason got to his feet. "Come on, Della."

They left Arthur Sheldon still sitting on the edge of the bed, shivering slightly.

From a phone booth in an all-night restaurant two blocks down the street from the hotel, Mason called the night number of Paul Drake, head of the Drake Detective Agency. "How quick can you get some shadows on a man in the Richmell Hotel, Paul?"

Drake said, "Have a heart, Perry. I can get competent men these days. But trying to get a room in a hotel . . ."

"How soon?" Mason interrupted.

"How urgent?" Drake countered.

"Damned urgent."

"Say half an hour."

"Okay," Mason said, "we'll compromise on twenty minutes. I want to have a man planted in the corridor on the fifth floor. I want him to cover room 511."

Drake's voice, more wide-awake now, registered a protest. "It's damn near impossible, Perry."

Mason said, "We'll talk over the difficulties in the morning."

"We'll have to cut the house dick in on it."

"Why?"

"Cripes, have a heart, Perry! You can't stick a man in the

34

corridor of a hotel at this time of night without having the house dick pick him up within an hour or so. That'll mean ten bucks, maybe twenty-five bucks.''

"Here's a tip for you, Paul. Room 510 is being vacated immediately. Your man can move into that room.''

"Okay, Perry, that's a break. The hotel is the Richmell, that right?''

"That's right. Her's something else,'' Mason said.

"What?''

"Don't go to sleep after you get your man on the job at the Richmell. I have another job for you.''

"I was afraid of that,'' Drake groaned. "What else?''

"I want you to find a horse.''

"Oh, sure,'' Drake said. "Something nice and gentle for Della to ride? Or would you like a little more spirited mount for yourself, Perry? I can get . . .''

"Skip the wisecracks,'' Mason interrupted. "We haven't time. The horse I want belongs to a fan-dancer.''

"A what?''

"A fan-dancer.''

"Say, look here,'' Drake said, suddenly suspicious, "you aren't stepping out with a few drinks under your belt, are you, Perry, just giving me. . . ?''

"Hell, no,'' Mason interposed, irritably. "This is important. The horse is a seven-year-old chestnut gelding, American saddle-bred, fifteen hands high, white star on the forehead, white right hind foot. The horse belonged at one time to a man by the name of Callender, who is a big shot. He has a ranch in the Imperial Valley near the Mexican border. He gave the horse to a fan-dancer who covered a catch-as-catch-can night club in Brawley. The horse was stolen while she was there, or it may have just wandered away. I want you to cover the whole Imperial Valley. Start looking for that horse. When you find it, keep it under cover. Have your men on the ground by daylight.''

"How many men do you want?''

"Enough to find the horse.''

"Hey, they'll find it,'' Drake said, gloomily. "My men are good detectives, but that doesn't mean they know one end of a horse from the other. They'll be so anxious to get home from that desert heat that every man I send down there will telephone by ten o'clock in the morning that he's found your chestnut gelding with a white star on his forehead and a white right hind foot. And then I'll have to go down there myself to see if it's the right one . . . Say, Perry, how the hell would I go about finding out whether the horse is the right one, or not? What name does he answer to?''

"I don't know his name.''

"Well, for the love of Mike, Perry, there are probably a million horses in the Imperial Valley and . . . Hell, Perry, when someone wants you to find a dog they tell you the name he answers to.''

"Just how would a horse answer?'' Mason asked.

Drake thought that over and then said, "I'm damned if I know, Perry.''

"I take it you don't know much about horses?''

"I know enough about them,'' Drake said, "to know that unless we get a better description than that you'll have two dozen horses by ten o'clock in the morning.''

"Not if your men are really on their toes,'' Mason said. "The horse was lost about a week ago. It will have to be a stray horse that has wandered into some ranch. It will be an American saddle-bred gelding, fifteen hands high, chestnut . . .''

"Yeah,'' Drake interrupted wearily. "I wrote all that down when you gave it to me the first time. I still claim that we'll have a whole flock of horses by nine o'clock unless I can get something more definite to go on.''

"Well,'' Mason said, "I'll give you something more definite to go on. Unless I'm mistaken, the horse will have a bullet wound.''

"A bullet wound!''

"That's right. If it isn't in the horse, it will be a bullet implanted in the saddle. The saddle is a nice, hand-tooled saddle made by Bill Wyatt of Austin, Texas. Now then, get busy and get your man on the job at the Richmell right away.''

Chapter 6

It was nine-thirty in the morning when Mason unlatched the door of his private office.

Della Street had the mail opened and sorted in three neat stacks on Mason's desk: the important pile, which Mason must answer immediately; the less important pile on which action could be deferred; and the third and larger pile which could be handled by secretarial answers.

Mason frowned at the desk. "Gosh, how I love to read letters. Mail is a wonderful thing, Della. Every morning it brings us a cross section of people's thoughts. People who have mysteries they'd like to have me solve gratuitously; people who have an axe to grind; people who want to borrow money; people who make suggestions about cases I've tried. They all follow a certain general pattern, and yet they have that peculiar something which springs from individuality. Those letters help me to understand people—and if you don't understand people you can't ever expect to make a successful jury lawyer—but they don't make me want to answer 'em . . . Heard anything from Paul Drake, Della?"

"He wants you to give him a ring when you come in. Says it's nothing important, just a routine report, and Arthur Sheldon is waiting in the outer office, nervous as a cat."

Mason's eyes narrowed. "Seems to have something on his mind?"

"So Gertie says. She says he's driving her crazy, walking the floor and biting away at his fingernails."

"All right. Let's have a look at Sheldon, Della, and see what's bothering him."

Della Street picked up the telephone, instructed Gertie to send Sheldon in, and then met him at the door of the private office.

37

Sheldon walked directly toward Mason. His hands were fumbling at the inside pocket of his coat as he crossed the office. Mason said, "Sit down."

Sheldon, like one in a daze, continued to walk over toward Mason, and by the time he had reached the corner of the desk had extracted a thick wallet from his inside breast pocket.

"Mr. Mason," he said nervously, the words all running together in his haste and anxiety, "I want to retain you. I want to get your representation. A general representation, a blanket representation—for Lois Fenton. I want you to protect her interests."

"In what?"

"In everything."

"Well," Mason said, "when she comes in at ten-thirty we'll . . ."

"No, no. Whether she comes in or not I want this to cover *everything*. I have some money."

Sheldon opened the wallet and began pulling out money. There were five-dollar bills, one-dollar bills, a few twenty-dollar bills, one fifty-dollar bill.

Mason watched him gravely. "How much money do you have there, Sheldon?"

"I don't know. I haven't counted it. I've been busy, raising what I could."

Mason nodded to Della Street.

Della Street's nimble fingers ran through the pile of bills. "Nine hundred and eighty-nine dollars," she said.

Mason's long, strong fingers began to drum silently on the edge of the desk. "Give him back half of it," he said. "Make him a receipt for the other half, Della. Have it appear as a retainer for Lois Fenton and for no other person."

Della Street gave Sheldon half of the money back, moved over to her typewriter.

"Date it the sixteenth," Mason said.

Della looked up at him in surprise, then motioned toward the daily calendar on the wall which exhibited a sign saying "Today is the seventeenth."

"The sixteenth," Mason repeated firmly.

Della Street dated the receipt the sixteenth, and handed it

to Mason. Mason signed it, gave it to Sheldon, said to Della Street, "Run down the corridor to Paul Drake's office, Della. Tell him I want complete coverage on this case."

"Complete?" Della Street asked.

Mason nodded.

She said, "I'll be right back," and vanished through the exit door into the corridor.

Sheldon said, "This is a load off my mind, Mr. Mason. You understand how I—well, perhaps I hadn't better say anything more. I'll be running along."

"Sit down," Mason said.

Sheldon became afflicted with the restlessness of great urgency. "Mr. Mason, you're a busy man, and I've got things to do. I'll run along. You're going to represent Lois now and . . ."

"Sit down," Mason interrupted.

Sheldon moved toward the door. Then gripped by the power of the lawyer's eyes and the authority in his voice slowly walked back to the big, overstuffed client's chair and sat down on the extreme edge of it.

"You checked out of the Richmell Hotel the way I told you to?"

"Yes."

"When?"

"Why right after you left, of course."

"Have another room?"

"I finally got one, yes."

"Where."

"791 East Lagmore."

"A hotel?"

"A dump."

"How did you happen to go there? Ever stayed there before?"

"No. I just saw the sign. I drove around in the cheaper districts. I knew I couldn't get in in the better places—not at that hour."

"What hour was it?"

"I wouldn't know. It was right after you left that I checked out. I got this room about half an hour later."

"You're certain you checked out right after I left?"

"Yes."

Mason looked at his watch. Sheldon squirmed uncomfortably. "Why did you give me half of the money back, Mr. Mason?"

"You're going to need it," Mason said. "You can go now."

A look of relief flashed across Sheldon's face. He started for the door. "Remember," he said, "you'll represent Lois." And then after a moment added, "No matter *what* happens."

The door check slowly closed the door behind him.

A few moments later Della Street opened the door of his private office.

"Okay?" Mason asked.

"Okay. You wanted Sheldon shadowed. That was it, wasn't it?"

"That's right."

"That's what I thought you meant," Della exclaimed with relief, "when you said you wanted complete coverage. Paul Drake had a man in his office who'll pick up Sheldon at the elevator. Why did you want the receipt dated yesterday, Chief?"

Mason said wearily, "I guess you'll have to call it a hunch, Della—or it may be just the cynicism of a lawyer who has seen too much of the human soul when it's twisted by the hands of destiny. The police might regard it as evidence if it were dated today."

Chapter 7

Ten-thirty came and went with no sign of Lois Fenton. At eleven o'clock Perry Mason's private telephone rang sharply. This telephone, which had an unlisted number, did not go through the office switchboard, but was a trunk line connected directly with Mason's desk.

Mason picked up the receiver, said, "Hello."

Paul Drake's voice at the other end of the line said, "We've found your horse, Perry."

"Where?"

"Ranch down near Calexico."

"You're sure it's the same horse?"

"Yes. The horse came wandering in to the ranch all saddled and bridled, with a broken bridle rein, as though he'd been galloping and had stepped on it. The horse answers the description, but the pay-off is the saddle. It's a beautiful hand-tooled saddle made by Wyatt of Austin, Texas, and it has what my operative cautiously described over the party telephone as some additional metal inserts other than those put on the saddle by the maker."

"A bullet, Paul?"

"Judging from his words and the tone of his voice, that's what I inferred he was trying to tell me."

"I want that horse, also the saddle and bridle."

"You've got 'em," Drake said. "My man put up fifteen dollars covering all charges and has the horse. Then he rented a horse trailer, loaded the horse, and is well on his way up here right now. He was smart enough to wait until he got out of Imperial County before phoning."

"Good work, Paul. Remember I want the horse, the bridle and the saddle."

"Okay, you've got 'em."

41

"Anything else?" Mason asked.

"Just a lot of routine."

Mason said, "Hold the line a minute, Paul."

He turned away from the telephone, squinted his eyes against the light of the window, once more made rapid, nervous drumming motions on the desk. Then he turned back to the telephone. "Any mark on the horse, Paul?"

"A scratch along the horse's left hip. I gather from what my man said it was probably made by the bullet before it embedded itself in the saddle."

"Okay," Mason said crisply. "That does it. Come on in here. I want to talk with you."

"Be right in," Drake said, and hung up.

Mason said to Della Street, "They've got the horse. Open the door for Paul, will you, Della? He's coming in."

Della Street moved swiftly across the office, stood waiting at the door, and as she heard the pound of Drake's feet in the corridor, opened the door and admitted the detective.

Paul Drake, lanky and loose-jointed, crossed over to the overstuffed leather chair and doubled himself into a position resembling a jackknife.

"Gosh, what a break!" he exclaimed.

"Finding the horse?" Mason asked.

Drake grinned and the grin lit up a lugubrious countenance. "Identifying the damn thing," he said. "It saves me a trip to the Valley."

"Give me the dope, Paul," Mason said.

"Well, I put three operatives on the job. I told them to hire men to help them in the Valley if they had to. I had visions of having to go down there to unscramble the mess. I was afraid each man would show up with a horse that was his favourite candidate, and I'd have to be the arbiter. What the hell is an American saddle-bred horse, Perry?"

Mason grinned. "Take a look at the one you've got when he gets here."

"To me," Drake announced, "a horse is a horse. Gosh, it sure was a break that we ran on to this one. My man hit it first thing. Of course, when you come right down to it, Perry, the fact that he had a saddle on when he got away gave us a real break.''

Drake waited for Mason to volunteer information. Mason said nothing.

Drake asked, ''How did it happen that the horse got *lost* when it was saddled and bridled?''

''I thought you didn't know anything about horses.''

''I know the facts of life. When you put a saddle on a horse it means someone wants to ride him. When you put a bridle on a horse it means the same thing. And that bullet-hole—well, let's hope we get the right answers before the questions are made official.''

''Can you depend on this chap who's bringing the horse in, Paul?''

''I'd trust him anywhere, any time with anything.''

''And is he suspicious about the circumstances under which the horse became lost?'' Mason asked.

''Put that 'lost' in quotes,'' Drake said. ''Of course he's suspicious.''

''What was the name of the rancher—the one who had the horse?''

Drake consulted his notes. ''A chap by the name of No-lan,'' he said. ''Wait a minute, I'll give you his full name. Frank Loring Nolan. Of course, Perry, when my man gets back we'll have a lot more detailed information. What I know now is stuff I picked up over the telephone in a hurried con-versation. What I *want* to find out from you is how to answer the questions that I'll be asked.''

''Nolan's place fenced?'' Mason asked.

''Gosh, Perry, *I* don't know. My man got the horse and, after all, that was the main thing. As soon as he mentioned that extra bit of metal in the saddle and the mark on the back of the horse, I thought it would be a fine idea to do our talking at this end of the line *after* he got here *with* the horse.''

Mason said, ''Paul, where can I get an assessor's map that would show the various acreages and the ownership in that part of the country?''

Drake grinned. ''Believe it or not, right in my office.''

''You have one?''

"I have two dozen. Talk about coincidences! A few weeks ago I worked on a case where I needed detailed assessor's maps of the Valley, so I had 'em on hand for the boys when they drove in. And a good thing, too, considering the hour you . . ."

Mason interrupted the detective to nod at Della Street. "Get the maps, will you, Della?"

Della Street glided out through the exit door and down the corridor.

Drake slid around sideways in the big, overstuffed chair, adopting his favourite position with one arm of the chair under the small of his back, the other one supporting his knees. There was about him a mournful look of extreme pessimism, an innocuous, self-effacing expression which in any gathering would automatically relegate him to the background.

Della Street returned with the maps and Mason spread them out on his desk.

"You want to find this man Nolan on the map?" Drake asked.

"That's right."

"Down somewhere south-west of El Centro, just north of Black Butte somewhere," Drake said. "Now this was the strip of territory my man was to work. Here we are. Down this road. See that patch there? Looks like forty acres— F. L. Nolan—that must be the place."

Mason studied the map.

"What is it?" Drake asked, leaning over, as Mason's finger came to a stop on an oblong etched on the map.

"The name," Mason said, "seems to be José Campo Colima."

"Sure," Drake said, "there are a lot of persons of Mexican descent who own land down there and . . ."

Mason looked up at Della. "Mean anything to you?"

"Why, yes, of course. That's the courteous gentleman who took the old Mexican woman who had been hurt in to see a doctor."

"José Campo Colima," Mason repeated, musingly, "and he has a twenty-acre place about—let's see, I'd say it was
44

about a mile and a half to the north of the ranch of F. L. Nolan.''

''You know this guy Colima?'' Drake asked.

''I've met him,'' Mason said, and then added significantly, ''and that's all. Come on, Paul, we're going to go call on a man in the Richmell Hotel.''

''Your car or mine?''

''Mine, unless we can spot a taxi at the stand down here on the corner.''

They found a cab waiting at the taxi stand and Mason gave the address of the Richmell Hotel.

As they entered the hotel, Paul Drake said, ''I've got a complete report on everything that went on here after twotwenty this morning, Perry. That's when my man got on the job.''

''I'll get it after a while,'' Mason said. ''Nothing startling about it, is there?''

''Nothing except that your man in room 511 seemed to be doing a land office business until after three o'clock in the morning. And you were all wet about the chap in 510 checking out.''

Mason, who had been striding across the lobby toward the elevator, abruptly stopped. ''What's that?''

''Five-ten. The party didn't check out until more than an hour after you telephoned.''

''Are you sure?''

''Sure.''

''Where was your man spotted?''

''Up in the corridor in a mop closet.''

''Did he have to square himself with the house dick?''

''Hell, yes. It cost him twenty bucks, and he had to plant himself in a mop closet. Then he finally got the chance to move into 510, after the other party moved out. The room clerk didn't want to rent it to him because there wasn't any maid service at that hour in the morning and the bed hadn't been made up and all that, but he moved in there anyway.''

''And covered the corridor from that room?''

''That's right.''

''Until when?''

"As far as I know, they're still covering it," Drake said. "I sent a relief down to help him about five o'clock."

"Well, we'll go to 511," Mason said, "and stop in and talk with the boys in 510 afterwards. You got a shadow on that chap who was in my office?"

"Uh huh. The guy reported on the phone a few minutes ago. Your man went to a rooming house at 791 East Lagmore and holed up."

Mason nodded thoughtfully. "Keep your man on the job, Paul. Okay, let's go see Callender."

Mason signalled the elevator operator. They rode in silence up to the fifth floor, walked down the strip of carpet along the corridor, and paused in front of room 511.

A cardboard sign dangled from the door-knob bearing the words DO NOT DISTURB.

Mason glanced at his watch. "Ten thirty-five," he said.

"He isn't going to like it if we wake him up," Drake said, in a low voice. "Remember, Perry, he was up until around three o'clock this morning seeing people."

"He isn't going to like it, anyway," Mason said, and knocked on the door.

There was no answer. Mason's knuckles pounded again, this time more authoritatively. When there was still no answer, Mason rattled the knob of the door.

"Take it easy, Perry," Drake warned. "You'll have the house detective . . . Oh, oh!"

The knob which Mason had been rattling clicked back. The door swung open an inch or two.

"Take it easy, Perry," Drake warned again.

Mason cautiously pushed the door open.

The room was in a weird half-light, as though some of the darkness of the preceding evening had been trapped in the room with the closing of the door and the pulling of the drapes. The odour of stale tobacco smoke and cigarette ends assailed their nostrils.

Drake, peering past Mason's shoulder, suddenly turned, made a panic-stricken rush for the door of 510.

Mason, standing in the door of 511, said, "Hold it, Paul. Keep an eye on the corridor."

"Come on out of there, Perry. Please! I can't tip you off in time in case someone should . . ."

Mason gestured for silence with a finger on his lips, stepped into the room, gently closed the door behind him, and clicked on the light switch.

The body of John Callender lay sprawled on the floor.

The man was fully dressed, lying on his back, the right eye all but closed, the left half-opened, leering drunkenly at the overhead light. There was no indication of a struggle.

A Japanese sword had been plunged into his chest. The handle and some seven inches of blade stood straight up, protruding from the body.

That which made the scene the more gruesome was the fact that Callender had apparently, with his last conscious effort, grasped at the blade of the sword and tried to pull it out of his chest. His right hand, rigid in death, was clasped about the razor-keen blade, and that blade had bitten into the fingers, down as far as the bone.

Taking great care not to touch anything, Mason detoured the red stain on the carpet and looked about him.

The room in which the body was lying was the reception room of a suite. Back of it was a bedroom which Mason could see through the open door. The bed was made up and had not been slept in. Back of the bedroom was a bathroom. Lights were on in the bathroom. The door was partially open.

Using his handkerchief so that he would leave no fingerprints, Mason pushed the bathroom door all the way open so that he could see no one was in the room. Then he gently closed the door again until it was in its original position.

A closet at the far end of the bedroom caught Mason's eye. Here the door was standing wide open. More than a dozen suits hanging on a central bar were visible through this open door.

Mason moved over so that he could see the entire closet. It was well filled with clothes, clothes which ranged from rough tweeds to a tuxedo and a full dress suit. A shoe rack contained more than a dozen pairs of shoes of different types.

Once more using his handkerchief so that he would leave no fingerprints, Mason opened one of the drawers in the bureau. It was well filled with shirts and neatly folded underwear.

Mason pushed the drawer closed, walked back to the parlour of the suite, again detoured the body and opened the door a crack.

Paul Drake was standing in the doorway of 510.

Mason raised his eyebrows in a silent question, and Drake nodded.

Once more using his handkerchief to protect his hands from contact with the door-knob, Mason stepped out into the corridor, pulled the door shut behind him and darted across to the sanctuary of room 510.

Drake kicked the door shut.

A man who had evidently been asleep had thrown off a light blanket and was sitting up on the edge of the rumpled bed. His coat had been hung over the back of a chair, his shoes were on the floor, he was wearing shirt and trousers. Another man, standing near the washbowl, held a half-smoked cigarette in between the forked fingers of his right hand, the smoke eddying upward. He was regarding Paul Drake with hard, startled eyes.

Drake said, "Do you know these boys, Perry?"

Mason shook his head.

Paul Drake indicated the man on the bed. "Frank Faulkner," he said, and then nodding toward the man standing up, said, "Harvey Julian."

Both men nodded. There was no attempt made to mouth any acknowledgment of the introduction.

Drake turned to Mason. "I'm going to have to report this, Perry."

Mason shook his head, waved his hand back and forth with the fingers open, a gesture of dismissal.

"I tell you, I've *got* to," Drake said. "Hell's bells, Perry, I've got a licence at stake. The smart boys amended Section 7578 of the Business and Professions Code to provide that in addition to all of the other causes for revoking the licence of a private detective, the Board could make a revocation for 'any other cause which the Board deems sufficient.' You

48

know what that means. They've got you where it hurts. And they don't like me."

Mason said, "Just a minute, Paul. I want to find out something first."

Drake shook his head. "Perry, I'm telling you I can't take a chance with it. We don't know what's going to happen here, and if I don't . . ."

He broke off as knuckles sounded on the door panel.

"Now what?" Mason asked.

"Oh, Lord," Drake groaned. "We're in for it now. We . . ."

"Wait a minute," Mason said, as the knock was repeated. "Hold everything, Paul. It's across the hall, on the door of 511."

Faulkner stepped to the door of the room, placed his eyes to the eyepiece of a portable periscope which had been so arranged that the opening projected slightly above the edge of the half-open transom.

"Room service," he announced curtly, in a half-whisper. "A tray with a pot of coffee."

Once more the knock was repeated. Then Faulkner said, tensely, "He's trying the door-knob. Going in. Okay, he's in the room now switching on the lights . . . There he goes."

They heard the sound of a banging door, of steps running down the corridor.

"If they ever find out I've been there they'll have my licence for not reporting it," Drake groaned.

"Who's going to find out if you were in there?"

Drake snorted, "Don't be silly, we're sewed up."

"What do you mean?"

"That house detective," Drake said mournfully. "He's got the deadwood. And right now they're notifying the Homicide Squad. We couldn't possibly get out of here without putting our necks in a noose. We're trapped—right here in this room. We could stay here all right until the thing blew over, if it weren't for the fact that when the police get to quizzing the house dick they'll find out I had a man on this floor; that the house dick took twenty bucks to let him hide in the mop closet at the end of the corridor, and then put him

49

in this room. That means the police will come here. We don't dare to get out before they come, and when they *do* come we're trapped.''

There was a moment of heavy silence. Then Mason moved over to the room telephone, picked it up and called a number.

''What's the number?'' Drake asked suspiciously.

''Police headquarters,'' Mason said, holding his hand over the mouthpiece of the telephone. ''Okay. Here you are, Paul. Report your murder if you want to. Just don't mention my name—not yet.''

''They'll already have the report,'' Drake said. ''That bellboy . . .''

''What the hell,'' Mason said cheerfully, ''there isn't anything in the Business and Professions Code that says you have to report it *first*.''

Drake took the telephone. ''Hello, headquarters? Paul Drake, Drake Detective Agency. I want to report a murder. Room 511, Richmell Hotel. The victim is a John Callender. I had men shadowing his room. A bellboy went in just now and discovered the crime, and . . .''

Mason's forefinger firmly pressed down the button on the phone which cut off the connection.

''What the hell?'' the detective exclaimed.

''The law says you have to report it. You've reported it. You don't have to visit with them over the phone. Hang it up, Paul.''

Drake dropped the receiver into the pronged cradle.

Faulkner, the operative who was sitting on the edge of the bed, said, ''For God's sake, will *somebody* wise me up?''

Julian, on duty at the door, said, ''We don't know a thing about it, Frank. We're covering the room, that's all we know. Don't listen to their conversation, if you don't want to.''

Faulkner said, ''I don't think I want to.''

Drake said, ''That's all right. I'm responsible for you boys and I'm holding *you* responsible to *me*, Perry.''

''Okay by me,'' Mason said, cheerfully. ''Let's have the works and have it fast. Faulkner, you're the one who came on duty last night?''

''That's right.''

"When?"

"I arrived here at about 2.16 or 2.17, and got on the job in two or three minutes after that. I'd figure perhaps two-seventeen and a half, if I had to get right down to a split second. For all-around purposes, I entered it in my notebook as 2.20."

"You got here pretty fast," Mason said.

"I was having a poker game in my apartment," Faulkner explained. "Drake's call caught me there. He said it was urgent and I jumped in my car and came down here. Not much traffic at that hour of the night and I made it fast."

"What did you do?"

"I looked around for the house dick. He wasn't in the lobby—probably prowling the corridors. I carry a hotel key in my pocket for jobs of this kind. I walked across the lobby jingling the hotel key, got in the elevator and went directly to the fifth floor."

"Then what?"

"I looked the place over," Faulkner said. "The boss had told me that room 510 would be vacant. I saw there was light coming under the door. I also saw there was light coming under the door of 511. I figured 510 hadn't checked out yet and I'd wait for him to get out. I looked around the corridor for the mop closet. That's the best place to wait on a job of this kind. I found it. Fortunately it was located almost directly across from the elevator and where I had a clear view down the corridor. I got in there. It was pretty cramped, but I could manage to stand up and get a squint down the corridor."

"You had this periscope arrangement?" Mason asked.

Harvey Julian said, "No, I brought that with me when I came on duty."

"What time?"

"Five o'clock this morning. Drake got me and asked me to come up here and spell Frank Faulkner in case there should be a shadow job turn up."

"Where was Faulkner?"

"I was in the room here by that time," Faulkner said.

"What time did you get in the room?"

'It's quite a long story,'' Faulkner said. "I'd rather tell it the way it happened.''

"Okay, let's have it your way then," Mason said. "Only remember, we haven't got much time. Make it snappy.''

"Well, as I say, I got on the job at 2.20. There was a lot doing in room 511. People were going in and out.''

"What people?'' Mason asked.

Faulkner took a notebook from his pocket. "You want absolutely everything in the order it happened?''

"Everything. But let's clear one thing up first. What time did you get into the room here at 510?''

"The man who was in it checked out at 3.02 a.m. I got in the room about ten minutes after.''

"How did you get in the room?'' Mason asked.

"Went downstairs and registered.''

"Your right name?''

"Yes.''

"Then you weren't covering the corridor between the time Sheldon checked out and you got into the room?''

"Now wait a minute,'' Faulkner said, "*I* wasn't, but the house dick *was*. That's why I wanted to tell it to you the way it happened.''

"Okay,'' Mason said, "let's have it.''

"The house dick caught up with me about 2.35. I made a mistake. He was pussyfooting down the corridor and . . .''

"Never mind that,'' Mason said. "What happened?''

"There was a little trouble for a minute. I showed him my credentials, told him what I was doing and he was pretty hostile. I slipped him a ten and that got him over his hostility. He told me he wouldn't turn me in, but told me to get out. It took another ten to fix it so I could stay here. I told him that I had a tip 510 was going to check out and I was only waiting for that to happen. I told him I had to keep the corridor covered.''

"Why did you tell him you were on the job?'' Mason asked.

"Told him I didn't know for sure,'' Faulkner said, "but told him I thought the boss was working on a case involving a hotel sneak thief. That made the house dick feel good. I slipped him the second ten and told him he'd get the credit for making the pinch, if there was a pinch, but that my boss would claim the reward on any loot we found in the place where the guy lived. That suited the house dick all right and we made a deal. He said he'd go back to hang around the desk and when 510 checked out he'd come up here and take my place covering the corridor. I could go down then and get the room."

"And it happened that way?"

"That was the way it finally worked out. Five-ten checked out around 3.02. The house dick got up here around 3.04 and I went down to the desk and got there just as the man in five-ten was going out through the lobby door, followed by the elevator boy lugging his suitcase. I pretended to the clerk that I'd been waiting around in the lobby all evening for a room and that I'd been promised the first check-out. The clerk didn't want to give me the room because he said they didn't have any maid service at that hour of the night. The last maid went off duty at two in the morning and she was only on duty for emergency calls. I finally convinced him I didn't care anything about that, so he let me have the room with the understanding that I'd take sheets and towels, make up the bed myself and put in fresh towels."

"Did you?" Mason asked.

Faulkner grinned and indicated the rumpled bed. "I didn't get *in* the bed. I just got *on* it. I put on clean pillow slips, that's all."

"Then you and the house dick must be buddies."

"We got along all right."

"What's his name?"

"Sam Meeker."

Mason said, "This is important. What time does he come on duty, do you know?"

"Sure. He comes on at eight at night and goes off at eight in the morning."

"Anyone on during the day?"

"I don't know. I didn't ask him. A lot of these hotels only use the house dick at night."

"All right," Mason said, "he's off now. That's going to

help. Now then, let's have a note of what happened in room 511."

"Well, just about the time I got established in the closet the guy who had 510 here came darting out of 511. He shot across the corridor, jerked open this door and went in."

"Do you *know* what room he came out of?"

"I *think* he came out of 511."

"You don't know."

"Not absolutely. It all happened too fast."

"All right then, you don't *know* what room he came out of."

"I *think* I know."

"It's your neck," Mason said. "Stick it out as far as you like, or keep it in. Which side of the corridor was the mop closet on?"

"On the other side from 511."

"On the same side as 510?"

"That's right."

"Then, looking down along the corridor, when the man went back into the room you say you think was 510, you didn't have any depth of perspective. In other words, you were looking right along a solid line of doors. How could you tell exactly which door the man entered?"

Faulkner said, "He went in 510. In the first place, the door looked like that of 510, but in the second place, when he opened the door, the oblong of light streamed out into the corridor and fell right on the door of 511. That shows the door was exactly opposite, and then when I went down to the lobby and 510 was checking out, I saw the way the man was dressed. He had on exactly the same clothes that the man had worn who came out of 511; a distinctive checkered suit."

"All right, what happened after that?"

"At about two twenty-two and a half," Faulkner said, "the elevator stopped. I clocked it as 2.23, but if you want to get really technical about it, it was probably a few seconds before that. And you should have seen the dish that got out."

"Give me the particulars."

"She was class. She had on a tight-fitting little fine-patterned greyish sort of skirt that hit her right at the top of the knees, and boy, oh boy, did she have legs and everything that went with 'em, and the way she used her feet when she walked! Seemed to just drift along over the floor.''

''Young?''

''Just a dish,'' Faulkner said, ''around twenty-two or twenty-three, maybe.''

''Blonde or brunette?''

''Auburn-haired.''

''Anything in her hands?''

''A violin case.''

''Go on,'' Mason said.

''She went down to 511.''

''Then what?''

''She knocked, waited, evidently heard someone tell her to come in. She opened the door and went in.''

''You don't *know* anyone called to her to come in?''

''No. I couldn't hear. Just the way she opened the door is all.''

''Better save the mind-reading,'' Mason warned. ''This is going to be a murder case. You'll be on the stand. What happened next?''

''She came out in just about ten minutes. I clocked her out at 2.32.''

''Still carrying the violin case?''

''Still carrying the violin case.''

''Then what?'' Mason asked.

''Then, at 2.44, a droop about twenty-six or -seven got out of the elevator. He walked down the corridor like he was going to a fire. He opened the door of 511 and popped in, and then he popped out and came down the corridor. . . . Well, he acted as though he wanted to run but didn't dare.''

''How long was he in there?''

''Ten seconds.''

''Describe him.''

''Droopy shoulders, thin, five seven or eight, a hundred and thirty maybe. He was wearing a brown overcoat, buttoned up.''

''An overcoat?''

"Yes, a light-weight gabardine."

"Hat?"

"No. Brown curly hair—a dime-store sheik, an under-fed wolf, fast on his feet, though. I put him as a half pimp or a tout. He had something to deliver, something he wanted to leave. I thought he'd phoned from downstairs and had a clear-ance, the way he popped into the room and then popped out. You know the way those squirts are. But, of course, he *could* have seen something that scared him—something on the floor."

"Better let the police do the speculating. He didn't come *right* out?"

"It depends on what you mean by that. It was ten seconds. I timed him."

Mason grinned. "Then he wasn't scared. Paul Drake beat that time by nine and four-fifths seconds. What else you got?"

"Then at 3.02 Sheldon came out and walked across to the door of 511. I thought he was going to knock for a minute, but he didn't knock. He just stood there as though he were listening and then he started down the corridor toward the elevator. He was looking directly at the door of the mop closet so I eased the door shut before he got close to me. I waited until I heard him go down in the elevator and then I opened the door a crack. After a minute I heard the elevator coming up again. I ducked back into the mop closet but this time it was Sam Meeker, the house dick. He told me 510 was checking out and he'd stay on the job and watch the place and I could go on down and register and get the room."

"You went on down?"

"Yes."

"Take the elevator?"

"That's right. Sam took the elevator up. The elevator boy was in the lobby lugging Sheldon's bag, hoping for a tip. Sam stepped into the cage and took it up to the fifth, gave me the nod, and I stepped into the elevator and took her down. There's only one elevator running at that hour. I don't think anyone knew the cage had made a trip—either Sheldon, the clerk, or the operator. I left the elevator, moved over into a shadowy place in the lobby and as soon as Sheldon was out of the place went over and told the Clerk I'd been waiting in the lobby with the promise of the first check-out. I told him the man who was on duty before him had made me the promise. The rest is what I've told you already."

"All right, you got into this room and then what happened?"

"Nothing."

"Nothing?"

"That's right."

"There's a sign DO NOT DISTURB on the door across there. When was that put out?"

"That must have been put out just about the time the house dick was taking over and I'd gone down to register," Faulkner said. "When I came back and moved into 510 I noticed that sign on the door. I asked Meeker when it had been put there, and Meeker said it was on there as soon as he got squared away and noticed what was going on, but Meeker is a bigger man than I am, and he had trouble fitting himself into the mop closet."

"When you came back up here, that sign DO NOT DISTURB was on the door?"

"That's right."

"That sign wasn't on the door when you went down?"

"Well . . . I don't think it was."

"Did you ask Meeker about it?"

"Yes."

"What did he say?"

"Said no one had even been near the door of the room."

"But the sign wasn't on when you went down in the elevator?"

"I . . . I don't *think* it was."

Mason turned to Julian, the other detective. "What do you know, Julian?"

"Not a darn thing," Julian said. "Drake got me about 4.30. I was in bed. He wanted me to drive down to the Imperial Valley for him and I told him nothing doing. Then he wanted to know if I'd come up here and take a job relieving Frank Faulkner here in the hotel. I told him that was okay by me. He wanted to know how soon I could get on the job and I told him I'd have to get some coffee and I should shave. He told me to put a razor in my pocket and come on up and I could shave here. I stopped in an all-night restaurant and grabbed a cup of coffee.''

''Get anything else?''

''No, I wasn't hungry. I just wanted some coffee. I got up here and—oh, I don't know, I guess it really was a few minutes after five, but we called it five o'clock in round figures because there was nothing doing, and I told Frank to roll over on the bed and take a snooze and I'd take over for a while. I was getting ready to wake Frank up when you folks came up. I saw you knock on the door and go in, and then . . .''

''Here's what we've been waiting for,'' Drake interrupted. ''It's the law.''

Through the transom could be heard authoritative voices. A door opened and shut—opened again. A man's voice said, ''Let's dust that door-knob for fingerprints.''

Mason turned to Faulkner. ''This woman that went in at 2.23 and out at 2.32. Give me a better description.''

''She seemed to me to be two-thirds stockings.''

''That might be a good description at that. What about the skirt?''

''It was some sort of a little black-and-white checkered affair, and there was a coat to match. It was sort of greyish overall but there were little black dots in it, or something. It gave the effect of a very fine plaid with some sort of tan-coloured stockings and straight seams and—I think she had on brown shoes.''

''What did she weigh? How tall was she?''

''Oh, around five feet two, or three inches. You can just visualize a perfect figure and that'll be it. She had auburn hair.''

''What's going on in the corridor, Paul? Have they posted a man on guard?''

Drake, his eye on the periscope, said, ''Not in front of the door. They're all in there. I've got to check in with them, Perry. Are you ready?''

"Give me another thirty seconds. Open the corridor door, Paul, take a look down the corridor."

The detective opened the door, looked down the corridor, then closed the door. "Man on guard at the corridor by the elevator," he said.

Mason moved over and picked up the telephone. "Bell captain, please," he said into the transmitter.

A moment later, when he had the bell captain on the line, he inquired, "Say, what's wrong up here on the fifth floor?"

The bell captain seemed apologetic. "The police are requesting guests who happen to be on the fifth floor to remain in their rooms temporarily. It'll only be for a moment or two. They're getting names and addresses of witnesses."

"Witnesses to what?" Mason asked.

"I'm sorry, I couldn't tell you. It's a matter of police routine."

Mason hung up. Something in the wastebasket caught his eye. He bent down, retrieved two oily cleansing tissues with some red on them. He slipped them into his pocket.

He opened the window, waited for a propitious moment, then scaled his hat far out over the street and closed the window. He crossed the room, opened the door, stepped out into the corridor and walked toward the elevator.

The plain-clothes man stepped forward to bar his way. "I'm sorry, buddy, you'll have to wait a minute."

Mason looked at him in surprise. "Wait a minute! What for?"

The man turned back the lapel of his coat and let Mason see the gold shield. "Just a little formality."

"What's it all about?"

"I wouldn't know, but the Chief wants to get the names of people on this floor and ask them if they heard anything last night. It'll only take a minute."

Mason said, "Cripes, they rented me a room without a bath and I want to go down to the lobby to the washroom. You can come along with me now if you want."

"I can't leave the place here. There's one on this floor, ain't there?"

"I guess so," Mason said. "Oh well, okay. How long's it going to be?"

"Not over five or ten minutes."

Mason turned back to the corridor for a step or two, then swung back to the plain-clothes man. "You don't know where it is, do you?"

"Hell, no. I just got here. It ain't as though you needed a blueprint. Look at the doors. It'll have a sign on it that says, MEN."

"Thanks," Mason said, sarcastically. "You're *such* a help."

"Cripes, I ain't a traffic officer."

Mason walked along the corridor, ostentatiously looking at each door until he came to the stair door. He opened that tentatively, looked back at the plain-clothes man. When he saw that the officer seemed to see nothing alarming in this, Mason walked through the stair door and took the stairs two at a time. There was no watcher in the six-floor corridor, but Mason went up to the seventh floor and then to the eighth, just to be on the safe side. At the eighth floor he pressed the button which summoned the elevator, stepped in casually and was whisked down to the lobby.

Mason paused at the news-stand, then at the travel desk, walked over to the stand marked THEATRE TICKETS, then stepped out of the door and on to the sun-swept sidewalk.

"Taxi?" a doorman asked.

Mason nodded.

Chapter 8

Mason paid off the cab in the six hundred block of East Lagmore Street and walked down to 791. It was a rooming house, the street frontage of which consisted entirely of a flight of stairs over which hung a somewhat dilapidated electric sign.

Mason ran up these stairs, found a desk, a register, a key rack with places for some two dozen keys, and a dome-shaped hand bell, back of which was a sign, RING BELL FOR LAND-LADY. Mason thumbed through the register, found the name of Arthur Sheldon listed as being in room number five and marked paid.

The lawyer located room five and knocked.

Sheldon opened it. His face showed surprise. "You?"

Mason entered the room, pushed the door shut behind him.

It was a typical cheap room with a white iron bedstead that had been repainted at least once with a cheap enamel. A thin mattress sagged in the centre. The walls were stained and soiled. The lace curtains had been darned several times, enamel had been chipped off the washstand, and one of the rungs had pulled loose from the straight-backed chair by the window. A rocker, stained a nondescript dark yellow, with a concave seat of imitation leather, tried bravely to give the room an appearance of livability.

Sheldon sat down on the edge of the thin mattress, which promptly sagged down so that the iron side of the bedstead caught him on the underside of the knees. He motioned to Mason to sit in the rocking chair, but the lawyer declined the invitation with a shake of his head and remained standing.

"I want to know what happened last night."

Sheldon's eyes widened in surprise. "What do you mean?"

"You know damn well what I mean," Mason said. "Let's quit beating around the bush."

"I've told you everything I know, Mr. Mason. I told you . . ."

"Who was the woman in the room with you last night?"

"Why . . . What . . ."

"Come on," Mason said, "who was it? Was it Lois Fenton?"

"What makes you think there was any woman . . ."

Mason took the cleansing tissues with their rouge smears from his pocket, tossed them on the bed.

"Yes, it was Lois," Sheldon blurted.

"Where was she?"

"In . . . you mean when you were there?"

"Yes."

"Hiding in the bathroom."

"She'd been occupying the room with you?"

"Don't be silly. She came to see me because she needed my advice. She had just gotten there a minute before you came."

"Try something else," Mason said.

"Honestly, Mr. Mason, that's the absolute truth. We were talking it over in whispers when you came. I told her that her husband had the room right across the hall, that at any time he might see her going out, or learn in some way she was there. It was an awful mess to be in. Then I heard your knock on the door and she was in a panic. She ran into the bathroom and closed and locked the door. I stalled around as much as I dared and then you put your card under the door and . . . Well, that's the way it was."

"Why did she come there?"

"Because she thought her brother was going to see Callender."

"Was he?"

"He had an appointment."

"Who made it?"

"Callender sent for him."

"What time was he supposed to be there?"

"Two o'clock in the morning."

"Why did Callender want to see him?"

"I don't know. Probably he wanted to put the screws on him to try and get some advantage."

"All right," Mason said. "I'll give you one chance to come clean. Give me the whole truth and give it to me fast."

Sheldon said, "That's it. Lois was scared stiff. She stayed in the bathroom and almost had hysterics. After you left, she cleaned up her face as best she could and I told her to get out. I said you'd told me to check out, and that we could meet in the lobby."

"She went out?"

"Yes."

"When?"

"I don't know the exact time. It was just a minute or two after you left."

"Go directly to the lobby?"

"Yes, of course."

"And how long after she left before you went down to the lobby?"

"I don't know, Mr. Mason. I didn't time myself, but I don't think it was over five minutes."

"Did you check out?"

"Not then. I went down to the lobby and . . . well, Lois Fenton wasn't there."

"Where was she?"

"I don't know. I assumed she'd gone out somewhere. I was worried about her. I looked around for a while and then came back to my room. Then the real explanation occurred to me."

"Which was what?"

"While she was in the lobby she must have seen her brother come in to keep his appointment with Callender. She and her brother went out and were talking. That was the only explanation that was possible. So I went back to my room and waited and waited and kept waiting, hoping there'd be a telephone call. Ten or fifteen minutes past two I became worried for fear Callender had intercepted her in the corridor and she might be in there with Callender. Callender didn't

63

know me and I decided I'd find out. I crossed the hall and knocked on Callender's door.''

"Wait a minute," Mason said, "that was a pretty late hour to be knocking on Callender's door."

"I know, but I knew he was up. I could see the light under his door and I knew that he was expecting Jasper Fenton to call on him."

"You were taking quite a chance, weren't you?"

"No, Callender didn't know who I was. He'd never seen me. I made up my mind I'd give him a fictitious name and tell him that I was looking for Jasper Fenton."

"What did you do?"

"I knocked on the door and Callender shouted, 'Don't knock. Come on in. The door's unlocked.' I opened the door. He seemed surprised when he saw me. I told him I was looking for Jasper Fenton; that it was *very* important I see him and that I understood he had an appointment with Fenton. I asked Callender if Fenton was there. He said he wasn't. I asked him if he expected Fenton to be there, and he wouldn't give me a direct answer. He kept asking me questions trying to find out what my interest was in young Fenton. I stalled him along, and then told him I'd wait in the lobby and meet Fenton there.''

"Did you actually go into the room, or did you stand in the doorway?"

"I went in. When he called to me to come in, he evidently thought I was Jasper Fenton. When he saw I was a stranger, he was so curious to find out what I knew about Fenton's appointment he wanted to pump me. He said to close the door as it was making a draught on him."

"How long were you there in the room with him?"

"Just a minute or two."

"Where was Callender?"

"He was sitting in a big, overstuffed chair. He didn't get up all the time I was in the room."

"Callender was alive and well when you left him?"

"Yes, of course. Why?"

"He's dead now."

64

Sheldon was open-mouthed with surprise "Dead! What killed him?"

"You mean *who* killed him," Mason said. "Somebody stuck him in the chest with a Japanese sword."

"Good God!" Sheldon ejaculated, emphasizing both words.

Mason said, "The police are going to start checking over registrations in that hotel. They'll find you checked out at three o'clock this morning. The probabilities are Callender was dead by that time. They'll start looking for you. You're in love with Callender's wife. You had the room across the hall from him."

Sheldon walked over to the rickety bureau, jerked open a bureau drawer, pulled out some shirts, underwear, neckties and started stuffing them into the open suitcase, which rested on the floor by the bureau.

Mason watched silently as Sheldon pushed clothing helter-skelter into the suitcase.

Mason opened the door, saw the corridor was clear, stepped out and pulled the door shut behind him.

Chapter 9

Mason left the rooming house, walked down the street rapidly for some twenty yards, then stopped suddenly as though he had forgotten something. Looking back over his shoulder, he sized up the neighbourhood.

It was a typically cheap, low-rental district, with dilapidated stores on the street level; above them rooming houses, the cheaper type of offices, flats and apartments. Half of the buildings in the block were one-story and there was only one three-story building in sight.

The man lounging in front of the delicatessen store might or might not have been Drake's detective. He seemed to pay no attention whatever to Mason, but stood there looking through the help-wanted ads in the paper. He was neither too well dressed nor too seedy; a man who had a gift for blending himself into his surroundings. The car, which was parked at the curb near him, was dingy in appearance, yet had no distinguishing marks which could readily be identified. There were no bent fenders, no cracked glass in the windows or windshield. The car was not dirty, nor yet was it clean.

Mason waited for five minutes, then Sheldon came out of the rooming house, carrying a suitcase, an overcoat thrown over his arm.

Mason kept his place until after Sheldon had turned the corner and the man who had been reading want ads had suddenly folded his paper, got in the nondescript car and driven away.

Then Mason went back to the rooming house, climbed the stairs, leaned over the counter, extended his flattened palm and smacked it down sharply on the button of the dome-shaped, nickel-plated bell on the counter.

The bell sounded its strident, unmusical summons.

After a couple of minutes, the door behind the counter opened. A woman thrust out an inquisitive, uncordial head, saw Mason, appraised him, smiled, raised her hands to her hair, came out and said, "What can I do for you?"

She was in the middle forties, heavily fleshed, and the body underneath the somewhat faded house dress quite evidently enjoyed the freedom of uninhibited motions which came with the absence of a girdle.

She was, however, not unattractive. Her face was full, but the skin was smooth, the complexion clear. Her face was well made up, and there was a friendly twinkle in her eyes as she placed thick forearms on the counter, leaned forward and smiled up at Perry Mason.

"Around three-thirty this morning," Mason said, "you rented a room. I want to find out if you rented another one at the same time."

The smile left her face. "Three-thirty this morning?"

"That's right."

She shook her head. Her dead-pan face gave no clue to her thoughts.

"I'm sorry," he said. "I don't like to contradict you, but I happen to know almost the exact time when this room was rented."

"Which room?"

Mason placed his finger on the register. "Arthur Sheldon. Room five."

"That was rented about three o'clock yesterday afternoon."

"You rented it yourself?"

"Yes."

"The man have any baggage with him?"

"A suitcase and an overcoat. Look, what's it to you? Are you the law?"

"I'm not the law," Mason said. "I'm a lawyer. I'm trying to find out something for a client."

"Well, don't drag us into it," the woman said shortly, the face still wooden.

"I don't want to drag anyone into anything. I'm trying to get someone *out* of something."

67

"Well, of course, that's different," the woman said, her eyes searching Mason's face. "Say, I've seen you before somewhere."

"Possibly."

"What's your name?"

"Shall we say Smith."

"I've seen your . . . I've seen your picture. You're Perry Mason, the lawyer."

Mason nodded.

"You *do* get people out of trouble, don't you?"

"Sometimes."

"When they've committed murders?"

Mason shook his head. "Not when they've committed murders. Sometimes when they've been accused of committing murders I've been able to prove they didn't."

"Well, that gets them out of it, doesn't it?"

"Very effectively," Mason admitted, smiling. "The man who registered wrote his name in your presence?"

"Yes."

"Can you describe him?"

"Well, let's see. He was young, that is, I call him young. Somewhere around twenty-seven or twenty-eight, I'd guess, and he had light hair and brown eyes. He's of medium height and weighs, oh, somewhere around a hundred and forty-five, I'd say, on a guess. He was wearing a grey double-breasted suit and I remember his overcoat was a very dark brown. He put it across the counter here while he signed the register."

"And the girl with him?" Mason asked.

"Say, what are you trying to do?"

Mason kept his eyes completely innocent. "Trying to find out about the girl who was with him."

"This isn't that kind of a place."

"I'm not suggesting she shared his room. I thought she was with him when he registered or that she may have had another room."

The woman shook her head.

"Perhaps she came in later," Mason said. "Rather a good-looking girl, quite short skirt, good figure, auburn haired, wearing a suit that had a pattern somewhat similar to a plaid."

68

"How old?"

"Twenty-two or twenty-three."

She shook her head slowly. "We don't cater to that class."

"She may have been all right."

"No. If she looked like that and got a room here, she *wouldn't* be all right. She'd either go to a boarding-house or a hotel. This is a rooming house. I try to keep it clean. I can't be responsible for everything that goes on but I know better than to rent rooms to dolls. No matter what they tell you, they'll make trouble for you sooner or later. I keep the place pretty well filled up the way it is and if anyone like that came in I'd tell her the place was full."

"You can't say a woman like that wasn't in here at any time during the evening."

"Certainly not. I don't stand at the head of the stairs keeping an eye on the corridors. I size people up when they come in. I do the best I can to run a respectable place but I'm not going to sit on the doorstep and watch everybody that comes upstairs. I'm not a chaperon. If there's any noise, I stop it. If there's anything offensive to the other guests, I get the thing cleaned up, but I don't snoop."

"Then this man Sheldon may have had a woman visit him?"

"Sure and what's wrong with that? She may have been his sister, or . . ."

"I'm not trying to find any fault with the place," Mason interrupted. "I'm merely trying to locate this young woman. It's very important that I locate her and in case it interests you, I'm trying to help her."

"I didn't see her."

"And you didn't rent a room to anyone like that?"

"One thing *could* have happened, since you're being so nice about it."

"What?"

"When I go to bed at night I sometimes leave a sign on the counter stating that certain rooms are vacant; that the price of them is three dollars; that a person can register and put the money through this slot in the counter, take the key off the board, go in and go to sleep."

"Isn't that taking a chance?" Mason asked.

"It is and it isn't. Rooms that will make you trouble are rented earlier in the evening—nearly all of them before midnight. After midnight it's usually someone that can't get hotel accommodation and is more or less desperate. I only have two or three rooms that I do that with. They're the least desirable rooms. I add a dollar to the price and I don't put that sign out until after midnight."

"And last night one of those was rented?"

"Yes."

"When?"

"I wouldn't know. I know that there were three one-dollar bills in the cash box under the slot in the counter this morning and that the key was gone."

"What's the name on the register?" Mason asked.

"That's the point, there isn't any name. That's why I didn't think of this room when you were looking at the register. Whoever took that room didn't sign the register."

Mason said, "Let's go take a look at it."

"You understand," the landlady warned, "it's probably a false lead. But if you're sure this woman spent the night here, that's where she'd have to be."

"I'm not *sure*," Mason said.

"Well, we'll take a look."

"She still in the room?"

"I don't know. Suppose she is—then what? Are you going to talk with her?"

"Yes."

"Not going to make any noise?"

"No noise, no commotion and no argument. I just want to see her, that's all."

"Will she be glad to see you?"

"She should be."

"Okay. Come on."

The landlady led the way down the corridor. Her broad figure undulated beneath the thin house dress. Sunlight coming through a window at the end of the hall silhouetted her big legs against the thin skirt. She stopped in front of the door of one of the inside rooms, glanced at Mason, then

70

knocked on the door. There was no answer. She knocked again, more loudly. When there was still no answer she tried the knob.

The door was unlocked. It swung open. The key was on the inside of the lock and the metal tag which was wired to the key jangled against the door as it swung open.

"Well," the woman said, "she's been here and gone. Slept here and evidently got out early this morning, perhaps before I was up. In any event, I didn't see her go out."

The room was furnished similarly to the room Arthur Sheldon had occupied but there was only one window in it and that window opened into a narrow air shaft. Mason examined the bed. The person who had slept in it either had slept very soundly, or had occupied it for only a very brief interval. The sheets were hardly disturbed and there was only one indentation on the smooth surface of the pillow, an indentation which indicated a head had lain there in one position, quietly.

"Young," the landlady said. "When they're older they sleep all over the bed. Only a young person can crawl into bed and get out again and leave it looking like that."

"A young person with a clear conscience?" Mason asked.

"I didn't say that. I said she was young. Damn few young women who stay here bother about a conscience." She picked a long strand of hair from the pillow, stretched it against the white sheet. "Auburn hair. Maybe it's natural. It's fine enough."

Mason moved over to examine the washstand. The oblong mirror over the bowl gave back a slightly distorted view of his face. The lines of the window on the other side of the room showed in a weirdly warped pattern.

The thin carpet around the washstand was dark where water had been splashed, and the woman, following the direction of Mason's eyes, said by way of explanation, "She stood in front of the wash basin and took a sponge bath. Women all do that, at least all the particular ones. I'd rather they'd do it than that they didn't."

She walked over to the bed, pulled back the covers, stood looking down at the sheets and said, almost musingly, "Make

71

this up nice and smooth and a person wouldn't ever know the sheets had been slept in. She was a dainty sleeper, all right.''

Mason examined the drops of water which were splashed on the washstand and which had not yet evaporated. There was a pale pink appearance about some of the globules.

''What are you looking for?'' the woman asked over her shoulder. She was making up the bed now, carefully smoothing the sheets and pillow cases.

''Just looking around,'' Mason said. He moved away from the washstand, walked over to the wastebasket, glanced into it, started to turn away, then stopped.

Something which had stuck to the side of the wastebasket caught a faint breath of air and fluttered so that it caught Mason's attention.

The lawyer bent over the wastebasket.

A few of the loose white streamers from an ostrich plume had been dropped into the wastebasket apparently while they were still wet, and had stuck to the side of the basket. Now that the ends were dry they were quivering with every little current of air like the leaves of a tree.

The landlady was carefully folding back the top of the upper sheet.

Mason quickly retrieved the few slender feathery tendrils with thumb and forefinger. As he did so, he noticed what had caused them to stick to the side of the wastebasket. There was a faint, but nevertheless unmistakable, clot of red at the base of the feathers. Apparently an attempt had been made to wash it out, but as the clot still remained the white tendrils had been cut loose from the ostrich-plume fan and dropped into the wastebasket.

Mason opened his wallet, slipped the bits of feather into the billfold, and said to the landlady, ''Well, I guess there's no use waiting for her to come back.''

The woman stood back and critically surveyed the bed.

''If she's young and she needs help, it's a shame you can't find her.'' She stretched the frayed bedspread taut and tucked it in at the foot of the bed.

72

"It is indeed," Mason said, and there was that in his voice which caused the landlady to jerk her head up and look at him sharply.

Chapter 10

Paul Drake entered Mason's office wearily.

"Well," Mason asked, "how bad was it?"

"Pretty damn bad," Drake said.

"What happened?"

"Sergeant Dorset was there. He wanted to get tough."

"He always does."

"Sheldon put the DO NOT DISTURB sign on Callender's door."

"You're sure?"

"The police are."

"How come?"

"Well, when they searched Callender's room they found his DO NOT DISTURB sign hanging in its proper place in the closet. When they searched room five-ten they couldn't find the DO NOT DISTURB sign. It had been there earlier in the day because the room had been checked by the maid when she made it up."

"Anything else? They get any of those other people straightened out—the ones who had called on Callender?"

"The woman who came in at two twenty-three had an appointment."

"You're sure?"

"Yes. The house dick stopped her at the elevator. She tried to pull a stunt of righteous indignation, but he demanded to know where she was going and she said she was going to room five-eleven. The house dick told her she'd have to use the house phone and get a clearance from that room. He went over to the house telephone with her and called five-eleven. When Callender answered, he gave her the phone. She said, 'It's me. I'm downstairs. The house dick made me phone. I'll be right up.' Callender's a regular tenant.

74

They gave him the breaks as much as possible. Anyone else might have had to come down to the lobby to see a gal at that hour. The girl gave her name to the house dick—Lois Fenton.

"Callender was a nut on his morning coffee. He didn't want to wake up until his coffee was there all ready to serve. He'd leave an order the night before when he wanted it. That's why the waiter knocked and tried the door in spite of the DO NOT DISTURB sign.

"Another thing, this Fenton girl had called on Callender earlier. A maid saw her leaving Callender's room at 2.00 A.M. Callender stood in the doorway and said, 'It's good-bye, then,' or something of the sort. He seemed pretty grim about it.

"The maid said the girl started for the elevator, then seemed to change her mind and went back and took the stairs. The maid would have reported it if it hadn't been Callender's room. He's a privileged character."

"It's the same woman, Paul?"

"The description fits her like a glove."

"So the police are nominating Lois Fenton, is that it?"

"That's right, with Sheldon as accomplice. And they've found something else, Perry. A very peculiar bloodstained imprint on the wall."

"What sort of an imprint?"

Drake said, "The police haven't exactly accounted for it yet, but from their description *I* think *I* know what it is."

"What is it?"

"It's the sort of print that would have been made by an ostrich feather fan that had been soaked in blood and then slapped against the side of the wall to get rid of the blood. A semi-circular stain with a lot of little lacelike fingers forming a more or less symmetrical pattern."

Mason pursed his lips. "How long have I got?"

"I don't know."

"Did Faulkner tell them I'd been there?"

"He hadn't up to the time we left, but the police were holding Faulkner and Julian for further questioning."

"They'll tell?"

"Hell's bells, Perry, they've *got* to tell! And I'm in a spot

75

myself. I have that horse coming up here and—well, the police are going to want to know all about the entire case and . . .''

Mason looked at him in surprise. ''What the hell has the horse got to do with it?'' he asked.

''Cripes,'' Drake said, ''it's part of the case.''

''What gives you that idea?''

''Why, you asked me to get the men on the job searching for that horse at the same time as . . . Say, *isn't* the horse a part of this case?''

Mason frowned at him. ''Were you intending to tell the police all about *all* of your business?''

''No, Perry, of course not, but . . . well, hang it, I'll have to answer their questions.''

''That's fine,'' Mason told him. ''When they ask you about a horse, tell 'em about a horse. Until they do ask you, don't tell them a damn thing about any horse.''

When the door had closed behind Paul Drake, Mason turned to Della Street. ''Got a pencil handy, Della?''

She picked up her pencil by way of answer, slid a short-hand book into position on her knee, and raised inquisitive eyebrows, waiting for Mason's dictation.

Mason said, ''I want to construct a timetable and get it in chronological order. What time do you suppose it was when we went to the hotel?''

''The Richmell?''

''Yes.''

She said, ''I looked at my watch when we reached the city. It was a little after one—about eight minutes, I think.''

Mason said, ''Allowing time to reach the hotel from that point, putting it in round figures, we'll call it one-twenty A.M. when we entered the hotel. This night-club waiter, Harry, was calling on Callender at that time. We don't know when he went out. Just start tabulating it, Della. Put one-twenty, Harry goes in. Then make a blank for the time he left.

''Now, the next time we know anything about someone being in the room is two o'clock, when the maid saw an unidentified woman, who may have been Lois Fenton, leaving the room. After that we have Sheldon leaving the room at about two twenty-one. At two twenty-three this woman who gave the name of Lois Fenton was back in the room again, and at two thirty-two or two thirty-three she was out. At two forty-four a young man was in and at two forty-four-ten he was out. At three-two Sheldon checked out. Type that into a time schedule, will you please?''

Della Street fed a small piece of paper into her typewriter and worked out a schedule:

1:20	A.M.	Harry, the waiter, into room
——	A.M.	Harry leaves
——	A.M.	Woman into room
2:00	A.M.	Woman leaves
——	A.M.	Sheldon into room
2:21	A.M.	Sheldon leaves
2:23	A.M.	Girl giving name of Lois Fenton enters room
2:33	A.M.	Leaves
2:44	A.M.	Young man enters room
2:44–10 sec.	A.M.	Young man leaves
3:02	A.M.	Sheldon checks out

She handed Mason the list. The lawyer was studying it when a knock sounded, and Gertie opened the door from the reception room, peeked in, and waited for Mason's nod.

"Come in, Gertie. What is it?"

"Gee, Mr. Mason," she said, "I didn't want to tell you this over the phone because I was afraid you might not see her. She's waiting out there, and boy, oh boy, is she *class*!"

"I take it someone has impressed you, Gertie."

"Impressed me," Gertie exclaimed, and rolled her eyes in an ecstatic expression. "If I had a figure like that—if I thought I could *ever* get a figure like that, I'd go without ice cream and butter and I'd never look a piece of candy in the face, and . . . Mr. Mason, she's superb, she's marvellous."

"And the name?" Mason asked, dryly.

77

"The name," she said, "is Cherie Chi-Chi. That's all the name she'll give. She's never been here before, but . . ."

"I'm quite sure we want to see her. Show her in."

The girl whom Gertie escorted into the office was the fan-dancer Mason and Della Street had met at Palomino the night before.

"How do you do, Mr. Mason and Miss Street," she said, smiling.

Gertie reluctantly closed the door.

Cherie Chi-Chi was wearing a suit, the pattern of which was a cross between the pepper-and-salt of a conventional tweed and a plaid. The skirt was tight-fitting and short. The legs were smoothly encased in sheer nylons. As she glided across the office, the short tight-fitting skirt did nothing to minimize her feminine charms. She extended her hand to Mason.

"*So* nice to see you again," she said cooingly.

"Sit down," Mason invited, glancing quizzically at Della Street.

The fan-dancer settled back in the overstuffed leather chair across from Mason's desk. She made a perfunctory gesture to pull the hem of her skirt down, then frankly crossed her knees and laughed up into Mason's face.

"Surprised?" she asked.

Mason shook his head.

She shifted her position in the chair. "After I saw you, I didn't put on any more performances at Palomino last night."

"No?"

"No. I came to town."

"Driving?"

"Yes."

"By yourself?"

"Harry was with me. You remember Harry, surely. The big waiter . . ."

"Yes, I remember Harry."

"You see," she said, "I had thought all along that you had found my horse, but when it turned out that what you had discovered was merely a couple of fans—well, then I had to see a certain party."

78

"Now wait a minute," Mason said. "Let's not have any misunderstanding. You're not a client of mine."

"No, of course not"

"And you're not really Lois Fenton?"

"No."

"Yet you've used her name."

"Yes."

"And you've called on me because you want something."

"That's right."

"What is it?"

She gave him a full-lipped smile. "You're very abrupt."

"Perhaps I am, but you want something, and I want to know what it is."

"Why so anxious?"

"I want to see what the pay-off is."

"There isn't any."

Mason settled back into silence. The young woman's fingers folded the hem of her skirt into little pleats, then straightened out the cloth again. "Would you," she asked at length, "feel that you *had* to say anything about those two fans?"

"To whom?"

"To anyone."

"That depends. What was the name of the party to whom you reported about the fans—and the horse?"

"John Callender."

"You know what happened to him?"

She let her left hand slide up and down the smooth expanse of stocking on the right leg, which was crossed over the left knee. "Yes."

"If you are trying to tell me anything, you had better go ahead."

She said, "I went in to report to John Callender. He'd hoped I'd get the horse."

"When did you see him?"

"Shortly before two o'clock this morning."

"Go ahead."

"Frankly, Mr. Mason, I told Callender exactly what had happened between us. I showed him the two fans that you

79

had brought to me. I told him I didn't think you'd really found the horse at all.''

''Then what happened?''

''He told me not to be silly, that you were pulling the wool over my eyes. He said you'd really found the horse, that these fans were just a red herring. He told me to get in touch with you again.''

''And then?'' Mason asked.

She said, ''I tried to get in touch with Mr. Callender about an hour ago and was advised that he was dead. Apparently he had been murdered. I thought I should come to you and tell you frankly what had happened.''

''Why?''

''Because I don't want to be dragged into it. Under the circumstances, I thought you might have some wrong ideas and tell the police—and the newspapers.''

''Callender was in good health when you left him?''

''Of course. A maid in the hall saw me leaving and John was standing in the door. He was waiting for someone. I thought perhaps I should tell you.''

''Why this sudden interest in me?''

''Because if you know the true circumstances you won't bring me into the picture. Otherwise you might—well, you might have a lot of wrong ideas.''

''So you decided to come to me?''

''Yes.''

''Your own idea?''

''Harry thought I should come.''

''And what did Harry suggest that you tell me?''

''The truth.''

''Have you told it?''

''Not all of it.''

''Well, why not go the rest of the way?''

''I was waiting for you to ask questions.''

''Tell me everything you want to tell me and then I'll ask the questions.''

She said, ''I've known Lois Fenton for about two years. Lois and I had both been in the carnival circuit. We both are the same build. In some ways we look a great deal alike.''

80

When Lois got married she didn't have any further use for her career. Her dancing had been very successful. I was just part of a girl show—but I had ambitions.''

"Go ahead," Mason said.

"I'd had a hell of a time, trying to get somewhere in the carnival girl shows. That's not much of a life. The movie scouts don't grab you out of those dumps. When Lois got married several months ago, I asked her if I couldn't take over. You see, the agent who was handling Lois had sold her on the strength of photographs and her reputation, and if I should take her name and step right into her itinerary, no one would ever know the difference.''

"You asked Lois if you could do that?"

"Yes."

"What did she say?"

"She told me to go ahead. We signed an agreement."

"Go on."

"That's all there is to it. I used Lois Fenton's name. I copied her clothes, made my hair the same colour. I also used the stage name of Cherie Chi-Chi. I used that whenever possible. Because, you see, that would be my own, and I wanted that to fall back on in case something happened and some day someone would say I wasn't Lois Fenton. I did all right for myself, but I'm not going to try and kid *you*, Mr. Mason. I don't think I put on anywhere near as good a performance as Lois did. But I got by. I got by very nicely.''

"Then what happened?"

She said, "Then something happened I hadn't really anticipated.''

"What?"

"Something I should have known would inevitably happen.''

"What was it?"

"Lois and her husband didn't get along. She left him."

"And then what?"

"Then, naturally, she wanted her own name back. She wanted to fill her own dates. She had a living to make.''

"And what did you do?"

"I couldn't simply surrender everything I'd gained.''

"So what happened?"

"Lois got a dating on her own in Brawley. She made a tremendous success there, and then she . . . well, she thought she was going to step right back and take over the bookings that had been arranged for me. I didn't think that was right."

"You went to Callender?" Mason asked.

"No, that was something else. Callender came to me."

"When?"

"Two or three days ago."

"Where?"

"At the little town I was playing before I went to Palomino."

"What did he want?"

"He said that he had a very valuable horse; that the horse had been stolen or had strayed away; that he thought someone had found that horse and that this someone might become confused because his wife, using her maiden name of Lois Fenton, had been keeping the horse. He said he was afraid that it would cause a lot of confusion. He wanted me to give him a letter and to sign another letter, using the name of Lois Fenton.

"He didn't fool me any. I knew it was a trick but he said he would stand back of me and see I didn't get into any trouble. He said he needed my help because the finder would know the horse had been in the possession of a Lois Fenton who was a fan-dancer and it might take a personal interview to get the horse back. He offered me two hundred and fifty dollars. I tried to hold out for three fifty. He wouldn't raise the ante, so I grabbed at it.

"Now then, that's the story. I signed these letters. I thought you had the horse. I was acting under Callender's instructions. If you keep quiet about the whole business we'll both be a lot better off."

"And where is the real Lois all this time?"

"I don't know. She tried to muscle in on my dates and I told her she couldn't. If the agent had any idea anything was fishy, we'd both be in the soup. We made it plain to her that she'd get into serious trouble."

"Who's the we?"

82

"Harry and me."

"Are you married to him?"

"No."

"He takes quite an interest in you?"

"Yes."

Mason began to drum with his finger tips on the edge of the desk.

"So," Cherie Chi-Chi went on, "I wanted you to know about the horse and about the letters I'd written and about how I happened to be using the name Lois Fenton. I had full and complete permission in the form of a written agreement from Lois to take over her name and go on and build up a career for myself on the strength of her reputation."

"Where is this agreement?" Mason asked.

"I don't know. John Callender had it."

"Didn't you have a copy?"

"No, it wasn't drawn by a lawyer. It was just a letter she wrote to me all in her own handwriting. We both signed it, but she didn't keep a copy. When John Callender wanted me to write you about the horse he said he'd have to keep that agreement for a few days if he was going to protect me. That was okay by me. He has a lot of political influence down there in the Valley. I gave him the agreement and he gave me the two hundred and fifty."

"Did you and Lois have any trouble over that Brawley date?"

"Yes."

"You saw her there?"

"Yes."

"How was she dressed at the time?"

Cherie Chi-Chi smiled. "She wasn't."

"I mean . . ."

"Oh, I get you. Yes, I copied her clothes. What the hell, I had a living to make. I'd been building myself up in the trade ever since Lois got married. I wasn't going to quit because she changed her mind. Her husband was rich. He could support her. I didn't have anyone to support me."

"Except Harry," Mason said.

83

"Don't be a fish," she snapped. "You are confusing the cart with the horse."

"What did you do after you left Callender at two o'clock this morning?"

"Went down in the lobby and then met Harry."

"Harry was waiting outside the hotel?"

"Yes."

"Then you went back again about twenty minutes past two?"

She straightened in the chair. Her eyes widened. "Went back where, Mr. Mason?"

"Went back to Callender's room."

She slowly shook her head.

"The house detective says you did."

"Why, no, Mr. Mason. Absolutely not."

"He remembers the occasion very distinctly," Mason insisted. "You went into the hotel, crossed the lobby and started up to the elevators. You were dressed very much as you are now and carrying a violin case. Naturally you caught the eye of the house detective. He stopped you and wanted to know where you were going. You said you were going to see one of the guests in the hotel and he demanded to know which one. You finally told him it was Mr. Callender. The house detective called Callender's room, then put you on the phone and listened to the conversation. You said you were coming up. Evidently Callender said to come right ahead. You took the elevator and went up. You arrived at Callender's room at approximately twenty-three minutes past two and stayed there for about nine or ten minutes."

She shook her head vehemently. "Not me, Mr. Mason. *I* was there at quarter to two. I left at two o'clock. I had no occasion to return."

"You say someone saw you leave?" Mason asked.

"Yes. There was a maid in the corridor when I came out at two o'clock."

"What did you do?" Mason asked.

"I started for the elevator and then changed my mind. I thought perhaps it would be just as well if I went down by the stairs. Hotels are sometimes a little fussy about girls going in and out at night and—well, you know how it is, Mr. Mason. I'm not entirely dumb. In order to be a good fan-dancer you have to have this and that, and these and those; and I don't try to conceal what you might call my business assets. I dress so that I'll attract a certain amount of attention. That's part of the business that goes with my racket. When a girl walks down the street of a town like Brawley, for instance, or Palomino, she wants to attract attention. Men whistle at her and talk about her and then go and pay money to see her put on her fan dance in the evening.''

"So you decided you'd go down the stairs?"

"Yes.''

"What did you do?''

"I went down the stairs. I walked down the four flights to the mezzanine, then crossed the mezzanine and went down the stairs and across the lobby.''

"And you didn't come back at two twenty-two or two twenty-three?''

"Absolutely not, Mr. Mason.''

"You can prove that, of course?''

"Of course. I was with Harry.''

"How long?''

She met Mason's eyes with steady calm. "As long as was necessary, I think, Mr. Mason.''

"You know that Callender is dead—that he was murdered?''

"Yes.''

Mason said, "I happen to know Harry called on Callender about twenty minutes past one.''

"Harry did? Oh, no, you're mistaken.''

"No. Harry called on him.''

"On someone else on that floor, perhaps, but not on John Callender.''

"On John Callender at about one-twenty.''

"All right, what if he did? John Callender was alive when I left at two o'clock, a maid saw him standing in the door seeing me out. She recognized both of us.''

"Anything else?'' Mason asked, refusing to pursue that subject further.

"Yes. I know that Arthur Sheldon had a room directly across the corridor from that occupied by John Callender. I know that Arthur Sheldon is—well, he's always been carrying the torch for Lois. I like you, Mr. Mason. I think you played square with me. I thought that I should tell you these things so you wouldn't—well, wouldn't stub your toe. You know what the score is now."

"Are you," Mason asked, "going to keep on using the name of Lois Fenton?"

"I don't know. I think so. I like it better than Irene Kilby. But why? My entire business career has been built up on that name. My contracts are in that name. My booking is in that name."

"There will, of course, be considerable notoriety—quite a bit of newspaper notoriety in connection with all this."

She cupped her hands around her knees, threw back her head and laughed. "Did you think that would frighten me?"

"I wanted to know what your reaction would be."

She looked down at her legs and said, "I photograph well, Mr. Mason."

"In other words, you'll welcome any publicity you can get."

"I didn't say that. I said that I photograph well."

Mason's unlisted telephone rang. Mason nodded to Della Street. She picked up the instrument on the desk, said, "Hello . . ." Then she said to Mason, "Do you want to talk with Paul?"

Mason frowned dubiously.

"Paul says it's important."

"Don't mind me," Cherie Chi-Chi said. "You can go into another room and take the call, or just be enigmatic over the telephone," and she smiled knowingly at Mason.

Mason picked up the instrument, said, "Hello, Paul. What is it?"

"Are you alone?" Drake asked.

"No."

"Client with you?"

"Not exactly."

Drake said, "The detective who found that horse is on the

way up with it. He telephoned from one of the outlying cities. He'll be in town in an hour. He's waiting for instructions on another line. What are we going to do about it?"

"Well?" Mason asked.

"Hell's bells, Perry, you can't park an automobile and a horse trailer out in front of the office building here, and you can't drive into one of the parking stations. What the hell does a guy do with a horse in a city? Where do you want the beast parked? You can't keep him in a closet."

"Can you call me back in half an hour?"

"I suppose I could, but this chap's waiting on the line for instructions. I used one of the other phones in the office to call you to see what you wanted done."

Mason said, "There are places that specialize in taking care of things like that."

"You mean you want him put in some livery place that's on the outside of town? Perhaps some riding academy?"

"That's right."

"Then someone will have to stay there to keep an eye on him."

"That's right."

"Okay, I'll see what can be done."

"Just a minute, before you hang up," Mason said. "The merchandise to which you were referring divides itself generally into two parts."

"What are you getting at, Perry?"

"Just what I said."

"What am I supposed to do—play guessing games?"

"That's right."

"Okay, I'll lead with my chin. It's a saddle horse. There are two things, a horse and a saddle."

"That's not what I had in mind."

"A body and legs."

"No. The same two things that are on a silver dollar."

"Head and tail," Drake said.

"Right."

"Okay, Perry, go on from there."

"That last-mentioned article," Mason said, "you got one we could use hanging around your office?"

"I haven't right now, Perry. I could get one in about four or five minutes."

"That may not be soon enough," Mason said, "but do the best you can."

"I'll have to have a description."

"I'll send Della down with it," Mason said, "and I don't think I'll ever bet with you again. You're too lucky."

Mason hung up the telephone, opened his billfold, took out a twenty-dollar bill and handed it to Della Street. "Drake wins," he said.

"Well, isn't *he* lucky!" Della said, almost too quickly. "I certainly thought he'd never win *that* bet."

"I didn't think he would myself," Mason told her, "but he's won it and we'll be good sports and pay up gracefully. Take the twenty bucks down to him, Della, with my compliments."

Della Street took the twenty dollars, started for the exit door in the corridor, then turned, and over the fan-dancer's shoulder flashed Mason a quick glance of inquiry. His answering nod was almost imperceptible.

Della Street slipped through the door. They could hear the sound of her quick steps in the corridor before the automatic door check had slowly clicked the latch shut on the door.

"Well?" Mason said to Cherie Chi-Chi.

"There's really no reason why you and I shouldn't be friends—good friends."

"Have you found me unfriendly?"

"Not yet. I think you could get unfriendly if . . ."

"If what?"

"If you thought that it would be to your advantage. I don't mean it that way. Perhaps I should say if you thought it would be to the advantage of a client of yours. I'd hate to have things turn out that way. I'm a good friend. I'm a hell cat as an enemy."

Mason said, "I'm interested in knowing what happened after you left the Richmell Hotel at approximately two o'clock this morning. Where did you go?"

She smiled at him. "Places."

"With Harry?"

88

"With Harry."

"Would you mind giving me the name of your agent?"

"Not at all. He's Sidney Jackson Barlow, in the Mayberry Building."

"And he's also agent for the real Lois Fenton?"

She said, coldly, "So far as professional life is concerned, there is only *one* Lois Fenton. I am she."

"He knows there are two of you?"

She shook her head.

"Do you intend to tell him?"

"If it happens to suit my advantage to do so, yes; otherwise not."

"Of course, you know there's no reason why I shouldn't tell him," Mason said.

"I've given you his name."

"I know, but I could have ascertained that in a very few minutes from any one of half a dozen sources."

She smiled sweetly at him. "That's why I gave you the name, Mr. Mason. If I thought you couldn't have found it out, I'd not have told you. However, Mr. Mason, I hardly think there's going to be any great amount of complications in the future so far as a circuit being burdened with an overbalance of fan-dancers."

"What do you mean by that?"

"I mean that *if* the house detective at the Richmell Hotel is in a position to testify that Lois Fenton called on John Callender at twenty-three minutes past two this morning, the police will see to it that Lois Fenton doesn't interfere any more with my fan-dancing schedule. And I think that's all I have to say, Mr. Mason. I don't want to take up any more of your valuable time."

"Not at all. It was a pleasure. Will you leave an address where I can get in touch with you?"

"Why certainly, Mr. Mason, any time."

"Thank you. That's fine."

"Simply call Sidney Jackson Barlow at the Mayberry Building and ask him where Cherie Chi-Chi is playing. Whenever you want to—shall I say—see more of me?" And with a smile and a quick lithe motion she was up out of the chair, extending her hand across the desk. Her firm, sinewy fingers gripped Mason's. "Thank you very much, Mr. Mason, and good day."

Mason moved over to the door which went out through the reception room, but the fan-dancer smiled, said, "If you don't mind, Mr. Mason, I'd prefer to go out the other way, the door which leads directly into the corridor. The one your secretary took when she went to pay Mr. Drake his bet."

She crossed the office, opened the door, gave Mason a cordial smile, and then her legs flashed in short, quick steps down the corridor.

Mason watched the door check slowly pull the door shut. Then he went over to his swivel chair, sat down and waited.

It was five minutes before Della Street came in.

"You got the message down to Paul all right, Della?" he asked.

"Uh huh."

"Paul do any good?"

"I think so. He wanted a description."

"You gave him one?"

Della Street laughed. "I told him that he didn't need a description. All he needed was to station a detective on this block and tell him to let his conscience be his guide; that if he found himself following anyone it would be the right one."

Mason grinned. "Specifically, what happened?"

She said, "I think Paul got a man on the job all right. He was frantically telephoning when I left the office. I went down in the elevator and stood by the cigar stand. That was to be my way of tipping off whatever operator Paul was able to get on the job to the identity of the person we wanted shadowed. He was to come to the entrance of the building, stand where he could see the cigar stand, and when this woman went past me I was going to speak to her."

"Was she suspicious when she saw you there at the cigar stand?"

"I don't think so. I stood talking with the girl behind the counter. When Cherie Chi-Chi came out of the elevators, I smiled at her. She came right across the foyer to tell me that you were just perfectly adorable. We chatted for a few seconds and then she said good-bye and walked out to the street. You know how the lobby of the building is at this hour of the day. People are hurrying in and out and going to elevators in a rush, but boy, oh boy, did *she* stop the procession.''

Mason said, ''That's fine, Della. Hold the fort here. I'm going to Paul Drake's office and help him make arrangements for board and room for a horse.''

Chapter 11

Mason had been with Paul Drake for less than ten minutes when Della Street invaded Drake's private office.

"Guess what?" she said.

"Another horse," Drake said gloomily.

Della shook her head, smiled at Mason. "Another fan-dancer. Lois Fenton. I think this is the real thing."

Mason scraped back his chair. "See you later, Paul." He started down the corridor with Della Street. "How's she dressed, Della?"

"In exactly identical clothes, has almost exactly the same colour hair, and looks very much like the other girl."

"How about Gertie?" Mason asked, grinning.

"Gertie is having kittens. She thought at first it was Cherie Chi-Chi back in the office. Now she's talking about going on a diet and she's trying to walk seductively, the way fan-dancers do."

"Let's have a look at her," Mason said, opening the door of his private office.

Della Street crossed to the telephone, said, "Send her in, Gertie." She hung up the phone and opened a stenographic notebook.

The young woman whom Gertie escorted into the room crossed the office toward Perry Mason and gave him her hand almost exactly as Cherie Chi-Chi had done.

Mason, on his feet, bowed, shook hands, and said, "My secretary, Miss Street. That's all, Gertie."

With obvious reluctance and a sigh which could be heard across the office, Gertie slowly closed the door and went back to the switchboard and the reception office.

"Won't you be seated, Miss Fenton? Miss Street is my confidential secretary who keeps things lined up for me and

92

I have no secrets from her. She makes notes on the things clients tell me, but you can trust her discretion.''

Lois Fenton sat down, found that the big leather chair made it impossible for her to keep her short skirt anywhere near the level of her knees, so she twisted to one side, doubled her legs with a swift, lithe gesture, and said to Perry Mason, ''I understand Arthur Sheldon spoke to you about me?''

''Yes?''

''He said that I was to come to you and that you'd take care of me in case the going got rough.''

''And it's getting rough?''

''You heard about what happened to John Callender?''

''Yes.''

''You knew he was my husband?''

''I heard he was.''

She said, ''I was preparing to file suit for divorce. What difference does that make?''

''No difference. You're his widow. If he left a will disinheriting you, that's one thing, except for your community property. If he didn't, you're entitled to a share of his whole estate.''

''I don't care about the money, only I'm thinking about—about my brother, Jasper Fenton.''

''Of course,'' Mason pointed out, ''the fact that there was bad blood between you and your husband makes quite a difference so far as the police are concerned.''

''You mean they'll think I killed him?''

''Perhaps.''

''Does that mean probably?''

''Yes.''

''Perhaps you'd better ask me questions.''

''Suppose you tell me exactly what happened last night, Miss Fenton, and then I'll be in a position to know more about it.''

''You knew that I was in Arthur's room when you called?''

''Yes.''

''How did you know?''

"I found cleansing tissues you had left in the wastebasket."

"I was in the bathroom. I could hear what was being said. I kept waiting for Arthur to say something about my being there. He didn't. I was terribly nervous. When you knocked, I thought it might be my husband. I rushed to the bathroom and locked the door. Then when I found it was you I was almost hysterical. I . . . anyway, I had a good cry there in the bathroom. When you left and I returned to Arthur's room I knew that my face was a sight."

"What did Arthur say?"

"He said I must get out of there immediately; that I was to phone him and let him know I'd made it all right."

"What did you do?"

"I stood there in front of the mirror making up my face as best I could, and told him that I couldn't go down through the lobby looking like that; that the house detective would think I was the fag end of a misspent life."

"Then what happened?"

"I knew that John Callender had a room directly across the corridor. I knew that he had sent for my brother Jasper. I knew that he was trying to blackmail Jasper and trying to reach me through my brother."

"Go ahead."

"Well, I left Arthur's room, closed his door, looked across at the door of 511 and suddenly realized that if I could definitely impress upon John that no matter what he did he could never get me back, he might cease his persecution of Jasper. It was one of those wild impulses that come to a woman at times and . . ."

"Never mind accounting for what you did," Mason said. "Tell me what you did. Give me facts—and be quick. Time may be short."

She said, "I crossed over to 511. I knocked very gently. John opened the door. I went in and had it out with him. I told him that if he tried to make any trouble for Jasper I would never speak to him again as long as I lived. I told him that the time had passed when he could get me to come back to him by blackmailing Jasper; that I was finished with him definitely, finally, once and for all.''

''Then what did you do?''

''I walked out of the room. Very sardonically, he held the door open for me. I think he might have tried to stop me leaving, only a maid happened to come along the corridor just then, so he said, 'I guess it's good-bye then.' I didn't say anything, but started for the elevator. He closed the door, and all of a sudden I knew I was afraid of him. It looked like a long way to the elevator. I remembered having seen a door marked STAIRS only a short distance from his room. I turned back, frantically tugged that door open and raced down the stairs.

''I ran all the way down the stairs to the fourth floor, then down to the third and second. Then the stairs ran into the mezzanine balcony around the lobby. There was a writing room there and I moved over to one of the tables as though I'd been writing, picked up a sheet of paper, folded it, put it in an envelope, walked down the stairs as big as life, pushed the envelope into the mail box and walked out.''

''Then what did you do?''

She said, ''I tried to find my brother.''

''Where did you go trying to find your brother?''

''Various places. I looked into some night spots where I thought he might be.''

Mason said, ''Now I want an answer to this and I want a truthful answer. I want it without any beating around the bush. Did you return to the hotel at any time after that?''

''You mean the Richmell?''

''Yes.''

''No. Definitely not.''

''You didn't return to call on Callender at about twenty minutes past two?''

''No.''

Mason got to his feet, began pacing the floor, paused, whirled, shot a question at her. ''You didn't return to that hotel lobby about two-twenty, didn't start for the elevator, didn't have someone stop you?''

She shook her head.

"This man was the house detective. He asked you where you were going and you told him you were going to call on a guest; he demanded to know which guest and you finally told him John Callender."

"No. Definitely not. Nothing like that."

"You didn't go to the telephone with the house detective, have the house detective call Callender's room, have Callender answer, have the house detective put the phone in your hands, have you tell Callender you were up there in the lobby and have him tell you to come on up?"

"Definitely not."

"At any time when you called on Callender did you carry a violin case?"

"No."

"Do you own a violin?"

"Yes."

"Have a case for it?"

"Yes."

"Where is that case?"

"It's with my personal things in the back of my car. You see, when I left John I was in something of a hurry and made up my mind that I'd go out and make my own living. I took what few things I had, my own really personal belongings, put them in the back of my old car and had my brother Jasper take the car to town. I rode my horse in. I knew the Valley Club at Brawley needed entertainers. I went there and got a job."

"And while you were there your horse was stolen?"

"Either strayed or stolen. I always thought it was stolen. I had him saddled and bridled. I'd been riding him. It was along about dusk. You know, it's hot down there and you don't ride an animal during the middle of the day. You go out in the evening. I'd been riding him just before it was time for me to go to work and when I finished it was touch and go as to whether I'd make it in time to come on for my first act. I climbed out of the saddle and asked the man who was boarding the horse to wait a couple of hours before taking off the saddle and bridle."

"Why?"

"Because, for one thing, the horse was sweaty and I didn't want him to get to water until after he'd cooled off, and then again I thought my brother might want to take a ride."

"Had he asked you if he could ride the horse that night?"

"Yes. There was a moon and he knew, of course, I had to be working there at the night club."

"So what happened?"

"I never saw the horse again. When I went out the next morning and asked the man if he'd taken off the saddle and bridle, he said no. He said he presumed my brother had taken the horse out for a ride and hadn't brought him back. I knew, of course, that was absurd. I found Jasper and asked him about it. He said that he went out to ride but the horse was gone. He presumed the man had unsaddled him, so Jasper just turned around and went back."

"Did you tie the horse up?"

"No. Just dropped the reins over the hitching rack. It never occurred to me that he'd wander away."

"And you think he did?"

"Frankly, Mr. Mason, I think the horse was stolen. There was opportunity for almost anyone to walk in there and lead the horse out if he had nerve enough."

"All right," Mason said. "That bring us back to your act in the Imperial Valley. What did you do after you left Brawley?"

She said, "That's a long story."

"I want it."

"From the first day I started out to be a fan-dancer, I made a hit. There's something about the way I put on my act. I try to be graceful and try to make the act a symbol of grace and freedom. I don't just prance around naked the way so many fan-dancers do. I try to really do something interpretive. You'll laugh, but I do. I'm free of clothes, free of conventions. People don't like always being a slave to conventions and . . . oh well, you can't put it in words.

"There was a girl who was built almost exactly the same as I, who wanted to be a fan-dancer. I'd known her in the carnival. She'd been one of the show girls. That's a pretty poor life for a girl. They have to take a lot of things—bumps

97

and grinds, and blow-offs. Of course, lots of places don't stand for that, but if you're a show girl in a carnival you have to be prepared to—well, I guess it depends on the carnival. But anyway, nothing made this girl car sick. She rode right along. But she naturally wanted to get ahead. This other girl, Irene Kilby, came to me when I got married, said that I had made a reputation for myself and was well booked up; that there was no need of just cancelling those dates. Why couldn't she take my name and go ahead and take over the bookings that I had? She'd use the name of Lois Fenton, but the stage name of Cherie Chi-Chi, and would get people to refer to her as Cherie Chi-Chi just as quickly as possible, and then gradually leave my name out of it."

"And you consented?"

"I got big-hearted and told her to go ahead."

"Anything in writing?"

"Yes. That was where I was foolish. I gave her a letter saying she could use my name and my bookings until I wanted them again; but at any time I wanted them I could have them back. We both signed it, but I didn't keep a copy. She has the letter. My husband was a witness to it. When he signed his name as a witness, he said that would protect me because he knew the terms."

"What happened when you left Brawley?"

"I saw no reason for going back and having to carve out my own career all over again. I rang up Mr. Barlow and told him I'd lost my booking schedule somehow, and asked him to please read it to me over the telephone. He read it to me and I wrote it down. Then I sent Irene a wire at the place where she was supposed to be, telling her that she'd have to be on her own from now on because I was taking over the next date."

"And what did she do?"

"Wired back that she'd used up all of the bookings I had when I left to get married, and that what she had now belonged to her and were for the most part in the name of Cherie Chi-Chi, and I could go get myself other bookings. She knew I didn't have any copy of that letter I'd signed and my husband wouldn't lift a finger to help me. He wanted me to make a flop. He'd even given her my favourite fans."

"What did you do?"

"I decided I'd fool her. As a matter of fact, Irene is no great shakes as a fan-dancer. She simply takes her clothes off and wiggles things around. She uses the fans as an afterthought and tries to make herself just as voluptuous as possible. That goes all right with a certain type of audience, but you have to remember that quite a few people in these night clubs are respectable; that is, they're putting on an air of respectability because they have their wives or girl friends with them, and they don't want to see anything that's *too* suggestive. So I made up my mind I'd simply move in on the next date, get there before Irene did and put on one of my shows. Then when Irene showed up and claimed she was the one who was entitled to the date, I'd let her go out in front of the audience and let the manager choose between us. I knew there'd be nothing to it after that."

"But you didn't do that?"

"Irene beat me to it. She was up in Palomino before I could get there. Her quote boy friend unquote, Harry, had fixed things for her. So, I decided to let her play that date out. I intended to go to the next place before I was billed, tell the manager that I'd finished up my other date early, and offer to go on as an extra attraction for a couple of nights if he'd pay me half price, or something like that."

"After you left Callender in the Richmell Hotel," Mason asked, "could you by any chance dig up an alibi for yourself?"

She shook her head.

Mason said, "I've got to keep you out of circulation for a while, Lois."

"Why?"

"Because you're hotter than a stove lid. The police will be looking for you by this time. They'll have covered the hotel registers, they'll have broadcast a description and every radio car in the city will be after you."

"It's a big city," Lois Fenton said.

"It's a big city, but you're just about as inconspicuous as

a mermaid trying to get on a street car. You have other clothes?"

"Yes."

"Where?"

"At the hotel where I'm stopping."

"Registered under your own name?"

"Yes."

Mason shook his head and said, "That's out. You have your car. Any clothes in it?"

"No. There's some junk stuff in the trunk but no clothes."

Mason, pacing the floor, said, "I can't afford to let you go back to your hotel. I can't afford to make it seem that you're running away from anything. They can prove flight as an indication of guilt. Flight would be the worst thing that could possibly happen. . . . I've got it! I'll take you to a place where the police won't find you, yet a place that is so logical that you would naturally be expected to go there in a hurry and without going back to the hotel to get a change of clothes."

"There isn't any such place," she said.

"Yes there is," Mason told her. "You're going to see your horse. We've located it in the Imperial Valley. I'm having it brought in."

Her face lit up. "Oh, that's marvellous! Tell me, Mr. Mason, is he hurt?"

"No. He seems to be all right except for a scratch. There's a bullet in the cantle of the saddle."

She said, bitterly, "That's one of John's frame-ups—the way he handles things. It's typical. It's part of some scheme. I don't think anyone tried to rob the place at all, and . . ."

"Never mind that," Mason said. "John's dead. The point is that you're very much attached to this horse, this . . . What's his name?"

"Starlight."

"All right. You're very much attached to Starlight. You come to my office. You learn that Starlight has been found; that he's being brought in to some stables on the outskirts of town. You also learn that he's slightly hurt. There's a scratch along the rump, perhaps where the bullet creased the skin.

It's only natural that you insist on dropping everything and rushing out to see the horse. After you see the horse, you'll be worried about him and be afraid that perhaps someone will try to steal him again. You'll want to stay with him. You should be a pretty good actress.''

"What does that have to do with it?''

"Hell's bells,'' Mason said, "I've given you the plot. Do I have to write your lines?''

Chapter 12

A high board fence carried in green letters a sign which read, ELITE-ACME CONSOLIDATED STABLES AND RIDING ACADEMY.

"That the place?" Mason asked.

Drake nodded.

He slid the car to a stop in front of a small building marked OFFICE. The three of them went in.

A man who was busily engaged in writing with big-handed awkwardness on a pile of invoices, put aside the pen and looked up as though he welcomed the interruption. "Something I can do for you folks?" he asked.

Drake said, "My name's Drake. I had a conversation with someone out here about boarding a horse."

"Oh, yes. I'm the one you talked with. The horse just came in. He's still in a trailer out there at the stables. The man didn't know very much about what arrangements you'd made. Now the question is, what kind of feed do you want this horse to have? I have some very fine oat hay and . . ."

"Oat hay and a little grain," Lois Fenton said, quite positively. "Not too much grain. I don't want him to get too hot—just enough to keep him on his mettle, and he should be exercised. If I shouldn't be able to get out here to ride, could you arrange for that?"

The man looked at her in appreciative appraisal. "He's thoroughly gentle?"

"Perfectly."

"Okay, I can arrange to exercise him."

"Not on roads," Lois Fenton said. "Just around bridle paths, and I don't want him raced."

"Sure, sure," the man said, soothingly. "I've got some good boys here. When I say exercise, I mean exercise. You folks want to go look at him now?"

"Please."

"Out this way," the man said, and opened a back door which led to the inside of a long, circular track back of the board fence. Over at the far end were stables, and in front of these stables an automobile with a horse trailer was standing facing them. A couple of men were engaged in unloading the horse.

As the party approached the trailer, they heard the booming sound of the horse's shod feet on the lowered tail gate of the trailer. They caught a glimpse of a tossing head. Then suddenly a horse pranced into view, pulling back against the bridle reins which were held by a lad who braced himself by thrusting the high heel of a cowboy boot down into the soft ground.

"Starlight," Lois Fenton called. "Here boy, here Starlight!"

The horse turned his head. The ears came forward.

"Starlight," Lois Fenton called again.

The horse answered with a low nicker.

"Let him go," Lois Fenton called to the man who was holding him. "He's all right now."

The man looked at the horse, then dropped the bridle reins. Starlight turned to face them, his ears still forward, his head up in the air, the bridle reins hanging down to the ground. Then, swiftly turning his head to one side so that the bridle reins dragged clear of his feet, the horse came mincing toward them.

"Look at how clever he is," Lois Fenton said. "He knows he's supposed to stand when the reins are dropped, but when he wants to go somewhere he just turns his head to one side so he doesn't step on the reins, and look at how he travels."

Lois Fenton stepped forward a couple of paces. The horse came to her, nickered again in throaty affection, nudged her with his head, then raised a soft velvety nose, put it against the girl's cheek and wrinkled his upper lip.

The man who ran the stables laughed and said, "It's her horse, all right."

"Where's the saddle?" Mason asked, walking toward Drake's operative who had been driving the car.

"In the back of the car," the man said. "And I put on new bridle reins. The old ones are with the saddle. One's broken off. I have the end of it."

"Do you want some money in advance?" Mason asked the riding academy owner.

"Brother, I want money whenever I can get it," he said, fervently.

Mason took out a billfold, handed him a fifty-dollar bill. "Take good care of the horse."

The man looked at the bill almost reverently, then slid it down into the side pocket of his trousers. "Sure, we'll look after him. He'll be all right. Where did he come from? Up from the Imperial Valley?"

"That general neighbourhood," Mason said. "In case the young lady wants to be near the horse for a day or two, is there some place around here where she can stay?"

"There's an auto court down the road about a quarter of a mile."

"Good place to stay?"

"Fair."

"That's fine," Lois Fenton said. "I'll stay there and whenever I want the horse I'll telephone. I suppose you can send a boy down with it?"

"Yes, ma'am. If it's no farther than that auto court, I can."

Lois Fenton smiled reassuringly at Perry Mason. "I'm all fixed," she said. *"Please don't worry about me."*

Chapter 13

The office Mason wanted was in a lofty building, where a general atmosphere of unconventionality clung to the elevator and the corridors.

The man who operated the slow, rumbling elevator cocked a weather-beaten eye at Perry Mason in a knowing leer, when the lawyer asked directions to the office of Sidney Jackson Barlow, booking agent.

"Fourth floor," he said, and clanged the door of the big elevator shut. "You turn right, and can't miss it."

He was a tall man who had once had blond hair. Now there were ragged fringes clinging to the scalp around his ears and the back of his neck. A long, drooping moustache hung dejectedly down from his upper lip.

"Marlow's got a nice filly stable," he volunteered.

"Has he?"

"Sure has. Known him long?"

"No."

"Nice guy. He'll use you right. Just don't ask him for addresses. Addresses are his stock in trade."

"How would he be for stag parties?" Mason asked.

"Best in the world," the elevator man said. "Here we are—fourth floor. Barlow's office is down the corridor on the right."

Mason thanked him and walked down the hallway. A door sign said, SIDNEY JACKSON BARLOW, *Walk in*.

Mason accepted the printed invitation.

The office contained a long row of chairs ranged along the wall, intended perhaps to impress the casual visitor that the business of this man Barlow was impressive in its proportions; that while this might be the slack moment of a dull day in an off season, the normal business of the office called for actors and actresses waiting patiently in a long line to see the very important Mr. Barlow, who was ensconced behind the mahogany door marked in gilt letters, PRIVATE.

As Mason entered the room, his keen ears detected the sound of a faint buzzing noise behind the mahogany. Evidently an electrical device under the carpet near the door had sounded a warning note in the private office.

Almost instantly a striking blonde, holding a notebook, three or four pencils and half a dozen letters in her hand, opened the door and made a great show of bustling efficiently to the typewriter in the corner. Her manner was that of one who is loaded down with secretarial business, and is fighting for minutes in order to keep abreast of her work.

"How do you do?" she said to Mason. "Did you wish to see Mr. Barlow?"

"That's right."

"What's your name, please?"

"Mason."

"What did you want to see him about?"

"Talent."

"You mean you want to arrange for some programmes?"

"Something like that."

"Just a moment," she said, smiling sweetly. She bustled into the inner office, carefully closed the door behind her, emerged after a matter of some ten or fifteen seconds and smiled again at the lawyer. "You may go in, Mr. Mason."

Sidney Jackson Barlow was seated behind a desk littered with papers and telegrams. At first glance it seemed that these papers had been piled in careless confusion on the desk, but a more careful observer would have noticed that letters were placed diagonally across telegrams so that the datelines were never visible. The walls of the office were decorated with dozens of autographed, professional photographs, men with profiles meant to be impressive, women whose pictures emphasized curves, legs and eyes, women with low-cut dresses and well-curved breasts, women with no dresses at all.

Barlow, a heavy-set, bald-headed man with thick lensed

glasses, devoted a cold-eyed appraisal to his visitor. "What was it you wanted, Mr. Mason?"

"I wanted to see you about some talent."

"Yes, yes. We have an excellent array of talent. Almost anything you want in the line of entertainment we can give."

"I wanted to see you in particular about a fan-dancer."

"Ah, yes. Something rather . . . er . . . intimate for a lodge gathering, Mr. Mason, or are you perhaps running a night club somewhere?"

"I wanted to see you about a particular dancer," Mason said. "A Lois Fenton whose stage name, I believe, is Cherie Chi-Chi."

The cold eyes instantly became veiled. "Yes," Barlow said, "what was it you wanted to find out about Miss Fenton, Mr. Mason? Of course, you understand our addresses are our stock in trade and . . ."

"It isn't that," Mason said. "I'm wondering if it has occurred to you that you have been guilty of fraud in connection with this dancer?"

"I'm afraid I don't understand, Mr. Mason."

"The Lois Fenton whom you have recently been booking is not the same Lois Fenton as the one you were booking six months ago."

"Why, that's impossible!" Barlow said. "Furthermore, Mr. Mason, I would like to understand your object in making such an accusation."

"I'm a lawyer."

"Oh!"

"Perry Mason," the lawyer went on, putting his card on Barlow's desk. "You may have heard of me."

"Oh!" Barlow said again, and this time there was a certain note of dismay in his voice.

"Do you see the acts that you book before you book them?"

"Yes, of course."

"You saw Lois Fenton dance?"

"Yes."

"When?"

"Why, I don't know, Mr. Mason. It was some time ago. I can't tell you the exact date."

"You were impressed by her?"

"A very remarkable fan-dancer, Mr. Mason. One who has a remarkable record."

"You have photographs?"

"Professional?"

"Yes."

"Yes, undoubtedly I have them. Did you wish to see them?"

Mason nodded.

Barlow pressed a button.

The door opened and the blonde stood in the doorway, a model of secretarial efficiency. "Yes, Mr. Barlow?"

Barlow said, "Get me the file of Lois Fenton."

She walked over to a steel filing case, slid it open and handed Barlow a folder. Barlow opened the folder, extended to Mason an eight by ten photograph on glossy paper.

The photograph showed a young, graceful woman smiling at the camera, portions of her nude body concealed by two ostrich-plume fans.

"Is that the only photograph you have?"

"No, we have some more recent ones that we're sending out on publicity. Elsie, where's that file of photographs?"

The secretary crossed over to a cabinet, opened a drawer, took out some two dozen photographs and handed two of them to Barlow.

Barlow handed them to Mason. They showed Irene in street clothes, the same short-skirted outfit she had worn to Mason's office, and they showed her without clothes, two very carelessly applied fans acting as costume.

Mason studied the photographs, said, "Just as I thought, Barlow. It isn't the same girl."

"What!" Barlow exclaimed incredulously.

"It's not the same girl."

Barlow took the two photographs, held them side by side, compared them. "Well, I'll be damned!" he said, under his breath.

The blonde secretary moved over and looked over Barlow's shoulder.

"How did it happen *you* didn't discover this, Elsie?" Barlow asked her, without looking up.

She said nothing.

Barlow put down the photographs, studied Mason carefully. "Who are you representing?"

Mason looked him squarely in the eyes. "Lois Fenton."

"Which one?"

"The real one."

"How does it happen I haven't heard from her before?"

"She didn't know what was going on."

Barlow moistened his lips with the tip of his tongue.

"Oh, nuts!" the secretary said calmly and clearly.

"Now, Elsie," Barlow said in a flutter of apprehension, "don't mix into this. This is a matter of . . ."

"Nuts," she said again, this time louder and more vehemently.

Barlow sighed with an attitude of a henpecked man who can do nothing further. He said apologetically to Mason, "My secretary handles a good deal of the clerical work in connection with the bookings." And, having delivered himself of that statement, sat back in the swivel chair and clasped his hands behind his neck, seeming to withdraw from the conversation by this gesture as effectively as though he had drawn a curtain between his visitor and himself.

Mason said, "And I gather that your secretary is in a somewhat sceptical frame of mind at the moment?"

"You're damn right I am," the girl said. "Don't tell *me* Lois Fenton didn't know someone had moved in on her territory. Those things just don't exist—not for as long as this has been going on. That photograph of Cherie Chi-Chi was taken three months ago."

"Miss Fenton," Mason said, "has been busy."

"That's *your* story."

"Now, now, take it easy. Don't offend Mr. Mason," Barlow muttered.

"She has taken an excursion into the realm of matrimony," Mason said. "Now she has encountered do-

109

mestic troubles and wishes to resume her profession. She finds that through your negligence, Mr. Barlow, someone has capitalized on her reputation, apparently with your connivance.''

"Okay," the blonde said, in a hard-boiled manner. "Come on, let's get it over with. What do you want? Out with it.''

Mason said, "I want to interview the person whom you are now booking as Lois Fenton, or Cherie Chi-Chi. You doubtless have her address.''

Barlow started stroking his sleek jowls with the tips of well-manicured fingers. "I think perhaps I'd better see my lawyer.''

"Okay, if you want to look at it that way," Mason said. "I thought perhaps I could keep *you* out of it, if it should appear that you have been the innocent victim of a misrepresentation.''

The blonde said, "Nuts to this lawyer business. Let me handle this, Sidney.''

She walked around the desk to sit on the corner nearest Mason, one foot resting on the carpet, the other swinging gracefully back and forth in a nervous arc. "What happens if you talk with this woman and it turns out she slipped one over on us?''

"In that case my client would be inclined to absolve you of responsibility.''

"Suppose this woman doesn't want to talk with you?''

Mason smiled and said, "That will be the measure of your good faith.''

"What do you mean?''

"You don't need to tell her anything about my errand. You can simply tell her that a man who is interested in talent is going to be here in an hour, and that you would like to have her available to talk things over with him.''

"That might make trouble," Barlow murmured.

"Keep out of it, Sidney," the blonde flashed back over her shoulder. "I'll run this. What kind of a party is it going to be, Mr. Mason?''

"That will depend on the circumstances.''

"Rough?"

"Certainly not. I simply want to get at the facts of the case."

"Why?"

"In order to protect my client."

"Look, you're not dumb enough to think that you can go to court and sue a fan-dancer and get any dough out of her."

"The situation could be rectified," Mason said.

The secretary's eyes narrowed. "In an hour?"

"Yes."

She turned to Barlow, said, "Well, why not?"

Barlow shrugged his shoulders.

"Okay," the secretary said. "We'll have her here."

"Thank you," Mason told them, and walked out.

From a phone in a drugstore two blocks away Mason called his office, using the unlisted number which rang the phone directly in his private office.

When Della Street answered, Mason said, "Be careful about what you say, Della. Is anyone in the office?"

"No."

"Anyone in the outer office?"

"A couple of clients who didn't have an appointment. I explained to them that you were out on business, and I didn't know whether you would be back at all to-day. They both decided to wait a little while on the chance you might be in."

"No one else?"

"No."

"No one been asking for me?"

"No."

Mason said, "I'm being shadowed, Della. I thought it was the police. The fact they haven't been calling for me at the office proves it."

"How long have you been wearing this tail?"

"Ever since I left the office after we returned from the auto court. I took the shadow on a journey—to see Barlow."

"What do you want me to do?"

"Just be careful *not* to act as though you didn't know where I was. I don't want the police to think I deliberately ditched this shadow."

"*Have* you ditched him?"

"Not yet."

"But you will?"

"Yes."

"Then what?"

"Then Lieutenant Tragg will go to see Barlow and ask questions, and be around asking questions. Tell him I told you I had to go out of town on business and that I might not be back until tomorrow night. Make it sound very casual."

"Okay. Anything else?"

"Just close up the joint at five o'clock and go on home. You may be shadowed. Don't notice it if you are. Remember to keep everything very, very casual."

"Okay. Anything else?"

"Be a good girl," Mason said.

"And be casual about that, I suppose," Della said.

Chapter 14

The hush of early morning still touched the desert, as welcome as cool finger tips to the forehead of a sick man.

Mason turned his car into Frank Loring Nolan's ranch driveway, swung out in front of the barn and then made a circle which brought the car near the back door of the ranch.

A bobtail dog started barking in the nervous excitable manner of a dog who expects to be silenced by his master and wants to get in all possible noise-making cacophonies before he is stopped.

The back door opened. A big man, whose stomach pushed out bib overalls, grinned amiably at the car and said to the dog, "Shut up, Butch."

The dog wagged his bobtail in recognition of his master's order and kept right on barking.

The man reached down to the ground, picked up a small pebble and threw it in the general direction of the dog, who promptly ceased barking, circled around past some shrubs and sat down in the shade where he could observe proceedings, mouth open, tongue hanging out.

The man walked over to the automobile.

Mason opened the door, got out and smiled a greeting. "Your name Nolan?"

"That's right."

"Mine's Mason."

"Glad to know you, Mr. Mason."

Mason said, "I suppose you keep pretty busy."

"We always find something to do."

"I don't want to take up your time, but I'm interested in . . ."

"Finding out about a horse," Nolan interrupted, the grin spreading over his face.

"How did you know?" Mason asked.

Nolan laughed. "That horse," he said, "—it looks as though that horse was gettin' famous."

"How come?"

"Darned if I know, but there certainly have been a lot of people asking about him. First some fellow came in and said he was representing the owner. He seemed like a nice-appearing young chap and wanted to pay whatever charges were due and take the horse along. He knew all about the horse, so I guessed there was no question but what he was telling the truth."

Mason said, reassuringly, "Yes, I know about him. He really was representing the owner."

"Well," Nolan said, "I'm the easygoing type. The wife is a little more suspicious. She took down the licence number on the man's automobile."

Mason nodded approvingly.

"A couple of hours after he'd pulled out," Nolan went on, "darned if some fellow didn't come in here that had a chip on his shoulder, and wanted to know all about the horse and all that. He turned out to be a police detective from the city. He wanted to know how I knew that the man was representing the owner of the horse, and I told him that he had a complete description and said he was representing the owner and that was enough for me. Then this fellow said, yes, whenever any slicker sold the Brooklyn Bridge to a sucker he always claimed to be the owner.

"Well, that started me thinking, and started me worrying a little bit. I went in and talked with the wife, and she said she'd taken down the licence number of the automobile. We gave that to the fellow and he went away."

"Then what happened?"

"Well," Nolan said, "last night the sheriff came down to see me and he asked me all about the horse, wanted to know where he came from and all that, and told me that I didn't need to be too loquacious in case people came around asking questions.

"So there you are, Mr. Mason. I just don't want to be too loquacious about some things."

114

"Well," Mason said, casually, "if you'll tell me the things that you can talk about and the things that you can't talk about, why then we'll avoid the things you can't talk about and . . ."

The man threw back his head and laughed. "Guess you must be a lawyer."

"That's right," Mason admitted.

"Say, wait a minute. I've heard that name somewhere. You aren't Perry Mason, are you?"

"That's right."

"Well, well, well, I'm going to shake hands with you all over again. I've read a lot about you. Never thought I'd meet you under circumstances like this. Say, why are you interested in the horse?"

"Generally," Mason said, "I'm trying to find out something that may help a client. There are some things that a lawyer can't talk about, you know."

Nolan said sympathetically, "If you'll just tell me the things you can't talk about, Mr. Mason, why then we'll know what not to discuss."

They both laughed.

"Tell me," Mason said, "when did the horse come here?"

"On the morning of the eleventh. About half an hour before daylight."

"How did he come?"

"Same way horses always come, partner. He delivered himself, walked right in on his four feet."

Mason smiled.

"How else would you expect him to come?"

"Shucks, I don't know," Mason said. "The way you're acting I thought he might have been eased down on the ranch with a parachute from some bombing plane."

"Nope, he came walking in a little before daylight, and the dog started barking. That damn dog. Never barks at the moon, or anything of that sort. Whenever he barks, you know there's something wrong, but he just keeps on barking until you get up and find out what it's all about."

"Well, I thought maybe a skunk or a wildcat was prowling around the chicken coop, so I got up and took my .410 gauge

115

shotgun, and started out with a flashlight. The dog picked me up as soon as I came out, and ran ahead to show me what he was barking at. And doggone, if it wasn't this horse standing there all saddled and bridled and nickering a little."

"And what did you do?"

"Took him into the barn, tied him up for a while, then took his bridle off, gave him some hay, and finally took his saddle off."

"See anything peculiar when you took the saddle off?"

Nolan pushed his lips together in a thin, tight line.

Mason said, "I take it that's one of the things you were told not to talk about."

"I ain't said a thing," Nolan said. "If you want to read my mind, I can't stop you."

"Did you go out and look for tracks?" Mason asked.

"Now, there's a sensible question," Nolan said. "You sound as though you lived in the country. Nobody else has asked me anything like that."

"Did you?"

"Yep. I went out and looked at tracks. The horse had come down the road from the north. He'd been on the shoulder of the road, where his tracks were left in the dust. Then he'd moved back on the highway. It was hard to tell just how long he'd been on the highway. I suppose I could have tracked him clean back by taking a little time, but right then I didn't see any particular reason why I should. I walked back for maybe half a mile or so, trying to see if there was any rider spilled along the road. I didn't find anybody, and by that time a few cars were coming along and I felt that if someone had fallen off the night before, and was still there, one of the cars would have picked up the rider."

"Anything else?"

"Well, I know the horse had been scared."

"How could you tell that?"

"Well, you see these western horses are trained a little different from the eastern horses. A good cattle horse will stand still just as long as the reins are down on the ground. For that reason cattlemen use a divided rein a lot."

Mason nodded.

"Now I tested this horse out a couple of times," Nolan went on. "I'd take him out and ride him a ways, get off of him and drop the reins just to see what he'd do."

"What did he do?"

"Stood just as though he'd been tied. Horses have got a lot of sense, Mr. Mason, and when a horse that's been trained to stand, the way this horse has, decides he's going to quit a place, it's because there's something in that place that he don't like at all. This horse had one broken bridle rein."

"Anybody else ask you about this?"

"Hell no, the other fellows that were here knew it all. You're the first one that's been here that didn't act on the assumption he knew all the answers and I was a dumb hick . . . And," Nolan grinned and went on, "you didn't do so good yourself the first minute or two."

Mason laughed. "Did you try frightening the horse to see how highstrung he was?"

"Well, now," Nolan said, "I don't know as though I'm supposed to talk about this."

"No one told you not to?"

"Nope. No one else ever thought anything about it."

"I can't see any reason why you shouldn't talk then."

"Well, you see, it's like this, Mr. Mason. I try to keep friendly with the sheriff down here, and I guess the sheriff is friendly with the police up there in the city, and I suppose there's some reason why they don't want me to talk about some things in connection with this horse."

Mason said, "Now let's be frank with each other, Nolan. If there was a bullet hole in the cantle of that saddle and the officers told you not to say anything about that bullet hole or about the bullet being embedded in there, I wouldn't want you to talk about it."

Nolan grinned.

"If, on the other hand," Mason said, "you wondered what could have frightened the horse and took the horse out and tried an experiment, I'd like to know what you found out."

"Well, I *was* sort of wondering."

"So," Mason said, "I take it that you saddled the horse,

117

put on the bridle, rode him out in the field, got off and let the reins drop and waited to see what he'd do."

"That's right."

"What did he do?"

"Nothing. He stood there."

"So then," Mason said, "you fired a gun. Is that right?"

"I guess you know something about animals yourself, don't you?" Nolan asked, due respect in his voice, "or else you're a mind reader. I fired a gun and that horse gave one snort and got out of there fast. I guess he'd be going yet if I hadn't closed the gate in the pasture lot."

"And the police didn't ask you anything about that?"

"Nope."

Mason said, "I think I'd like to meet your wife."

Nolan said, "She's sort of suspicious of strangers."

"I'd like to meet her just the same."

"Come on in."

Nolan led the way in through the back door of the house into a kitchen fragrant with the aroma of cooking. A thin, parchment-faced woman stood over by the sink washing dishes.

"This is my wife," Nolan said. "This is Mr. Mason."

She looked up, dried her hands on a towel, glanced at Mason suspiciously, smiled, walked over and extended her hand. "How do you do," she said.

"I'm pleased to meet you," Mason told her. "Your husband tells me you're the suspicious member of the family."

Her thin lips formed a straight line across her face. Her eyes snapped. "He's always saying things like that."

"Are you?"

"Well, somebody has to look out for things around here. The way Frank Nolan is, you'd think everybody in the world was a lodge brother, or something. He'd give them the shirt off his back. He thinks everybody's honest as the day is long."

Mason gravely took a billfold from his pocket, took out a fifty-dollar bill, handed it to Mrs. Nolan.

"What's that?" she asked.

"That," Mason said, "is a little encouragement to you to be suspicious."

"I don't get it."

Mason said, "Your husband is a loquacious, gregarious sort of chap. He's friendly with people."

"Too friendly. What's the money for?"

Mason said, "In case anyone else comes to ask questions about the horse, *you* might do the talking."

Nolan laughed. "I'm afraid there wouldn't be much talking done. She . . ."

"You keep out of this, Frank Nolan," his wife snapped. "I'm handling it. I guess if this man wants to pay me to keep you from talking, I'm going to try to earn the money. What don't you want him to talk about?"

"Anything," Mason said.

"Well," Mrs. Nolan said, "I guess that's a pretty easy way to earn five dollars. I'll keep him shut up."

"That's not a five-dollar bill," Mason said.

"It isn't?"

Mason shook his head.

She moved over and held it up to the light, looked at it, and then suddenly said, "Oh my God! It's fifty!"

Mason smiled at her incredulous surprise, shook hands with Frank Nolan, said, "Thanks a lot," and headed his car north, the bobtailed dog racing along snapping at his front wheel until the car hit the paved road.

A little over a mile and a half to the north, Mason turned in where a mailbox had the name "Campo."

An old Mexican woman, whose right arm was in a sling, walked slowly along the wide porch of an unpainted house, entered through a door and disappeared.

José Campo came up to the car. "Good morning," he said. "Is there something I can do for you?"

Mason said, "I wonder if you recognize me?"

"I . . . Señor, I have seen your face somewhere before, but I can't tell you where it was."

Mason said, "We came to inquire about the woman with the broken arm. We're from the insurance company."

"Señor, please give it no thought whatever," Campo said,

moving his hands in a gesture of dismissal. "It is nothing! I have made no claim. There is no insurance."

"But the other man had insurance."

"No, no, no, Señor. It is all right. We claim nothing."

Mason said, "The arm is getting along all right?"

"The doctor says it is all right."

"What doctor did you take her to?" Mason asked.

"A doctor in Redlands."

"Why go all the way to Redlands?"

"There are good doctors in Redlands."

"Some of the best," Mason agreed, "but why go all the way to Redlands?"

"She wanted it, Señor."

Mason said, "All right. Now tell me about the horse."

"About the horse . . . About . . . Ah, yes, it is the Señor who was on the highway at the time of the accident. That is right, the Señor Mason. Ah, yes, I remember now."

"And I want to know about the horse Callender gave you to keep for him," Mason said.

"No, no, no, it was not Callender. The other man."

"What other man?"

"The beeg one."

Mason said, "You know the fan-dancer, Cherie Chi-Chi?"

"But yes, of course. She came to us with this man about the horse and—oh, there was much trouble over that horse."

"Now, let's get the thing straight," Mason said. "Begin at the beginning and tell me about it."

"It was the day of the accident—that was a most unfortunate day."

"What happened?"

"It started when this man and the Cherie Chi-Chi, the fan-dancer, came to the ranch with the horse."

"How did they bring the horse to the ranch?"

"It was night. The beeg man is riding the horse. That is all I know."

"And Cherie Chi-Chi, the fan-dancer?"

"She came in the automobile, driving very slowly along behind the horse. It was night. First I can hear the clump, clump, clump, clump, clump of the horse on the pavement.

Then there is the sound of an automobile going very slow. Then lights shine on my house and these people come here. They are very nice people, and they want me to keep the horse for a few days. I am to keep him in the stable where no one will see him, and I am to take very good care of the saddle and of the bridle."

"Go on."

"And they pay me well. Oh, they pay me very well indeed, Señor. Of that there can be no complaint."

"Then what happened?"

"Then on this day, this day of the accident . . ."

"Wednesday, the eleventh?" Mason asked.

"I believe so. It is a Wednesday. Yes, I think it is the eleventh."

"And what happened?"

"The man telephones me. I am to put the saddle and the bridle on the horse and have him ready."

"Ready for what?"

"That I do not know," Campo said. "Simply I am told to have the horse saddled and bridled in the night and leave the saddle and the bridle on."

"And what else?"

"I am told that if questions are asked me about the horse I am to say that he came to the ranch; that he had the saddle and the bridle just as I have put them on this night; that I am afraid perhaps I am going to get into trouble so I have decided to put on the saddle and bridle and take the horse in to the sheriff."

"All right, what happened?"

"I have the saddle and the bridle on the horse and then the thing happens. Not that night, but in the morning."

"What?"

"It is early. It is not yet daylight and there is much noise among the chickens. It is a coyote that is very, very smart. I have had trouble with him before. He comes always long before daylight.

"My aunt, Maria Gonzales, she is a light sleeper and she wakens me. I hear the noise in the chicken coop and I take the shotgun. I run out of the back door with a flashlight. I hold the flashlight and see the two eyes of the coyote and I shoot the gun.''

''And what happened?''

''I miss the coyote and the horse runs away.''

''Where did he go?''

''That I do not know. I think that he certainly will not go far. It is dark and I am chasing after the coyote. Then I think that when it is daylight I will get the horse. One can do nothing wandering after a horse in the nighttime. I have missed the coyote. He is a devil, that one. Too smart.''

''So you let the horse go?''

''No, no, Señor! I did not let him go! I went back to bed. I am waiting for daylight to hunt for the horse.''

''And then what happens?''

''It is this way,'' Campo explained. ''This man, this one who made the arrangements for the horse, I think his name is Harry. Yes, that is right. It is Harry. The last name is—ah yes, I have it. The last name is Cogswell—Harry Cogswell. He wrote it down for me on paper. Harry Cogswell. That is right; that is the name. Harry Cogswell telephoned. I am to take the horse next day to the sheriff. And I am also to take two fans that this girl left on the ranch when she was here.''

''All right,'' Mason said. ''What about the fans?''

''I ask Harry about the fans and he says that I am to deliver the fans to him at Brawley. The horse is to go to the sheriff. But the horse, he is now gone. When it is daylight I do not find him anywhere.

''That horse, he will stand for hours with the reins down on the ground—stand still as though he is tied. I am expecting to find him standing in the driveway, perhaps as far as the gate, but, Señor, what could I do? It comes daylight and the horse is not in sight.''

''All right, what *did* you do?''

''So I have my aunt, Maria Gonzales, take these fans to deliver to this man, Harry, in Brawley, and I go to look for the horse.''

''Did you find him?''

''That I do not do, Señor. I dare not ask questions, because Harry has told me that the horse is secret—he is to be kept without saying anything to anyone.''

"Couldn't you track him?"

"Certainly I track him. I track him down the road. He is travelling with his reins dragging, and then he finds an open gate and wanders off into the field, and yet he is not in the field. There is another open gate at the far end of the field, and then stubble, and then more roads, but I do not find his tracks anymore. He is gone."

"So what did you do?"

"So when I cannot find him, I do not know what to do. I think I can find him by asking questions of neighbours: but is it permitted to ask questions of neighbours? That is what I do not know."

"Go ahead," Mason said.

"I know that my aunt, Maria Gonzales, is going to see this man, Harry, and I decide that I must go very quick to see this man Harry and ask if it is permitted to ask questions."

"So what happened?"

"So I am driving very fast to overtake my aunt, Maria Gonzales, and—well, you know the rest. There is the accident. She has the broken arm."

"And the fans?"

"I swear to you, Señor, that I did not steal those fans, nor did Maria Gonzales steal those fans. We are honest people. We are poor, but we do not steal. Those fans were taken from the car of my aunt, I swear that to you, Señor. They were in the trunk and my aunt Maria had been very careful to put newspapers in the trunk so that the fans would not get dirty."

"What about Harry?"

"He is very angry, that one! He thinks I have stolen the fans. He says I am too lazy even to keep the horse. There is much trouble. He says it is not permitted to ask questions. It is a very unlucky day."

Mason said, "That piece of paper that the man gave you with his name on it. You have that?"

"No, it is gone."

"Could you find it?"

"No, Señor, I could not find it."

"But his name is Harry Cogswell and you would know him if you saw him again?"

"That is most certain."

Mason shook hands. "It will be well for you to remember what happened," he said.

Chapter 15

It was early afternoon when Mason stopped his car in front of the auto court where he had left Lois Fenton the previous afternoon.

There was about the place that atmosphere of drowsy dejection which clings to auto camps during the middle of the day, when out-going guests have long since departed, when newcomers are still pushing down the throttle many weary miles from their destination.

Mason ran lightly up the steps of the little cottage that had been rented to Lois Fenton and tapped on the door.

"Who is it?"

"Mason. Are you decent?"

Lois Fenton opened the door. "What's new?" she asked.

Mason said, "You're looking better. How did you sleep?"

"Off and on."

"Not too good?"

"No."

Mason said, "You're going to be arrested."

"When?"

"Probably pretty soon. The police have traced your horse. They'll find the horse and you within a few hours. It might be better for you to get in circulation. Act as any woman in your situation would and let them nab you."

"How did they find out about the horse?"

"They covered the valley. They found the man who was keeping him."

"Is—is Jasper mixed up in it?"

"I think I can pin the horse on Irene and her boy friend, Harry."

"What do you want me to do?"

"You might begin by telling me the truth."

125

"About what?"

"About that rooming house on East Lagmore."

She bit her lip.

"Don't cry," Mason said impatiently. "Talk."

"I don't cry, ever."

"I thought you were getting ready to."

"No, I never cry."

"Talk then."

"Arthur told me that I must never tell anyone, not even you, about that."

Mason said, "When Sheldon left the hotel, he went to a rooming house at 791 East Lagmore. He registered there. Now, the strange thing is that he had registered there earlier in the day, long before he knew that he was going to have to check out of the hotel. Do you know *why* he did that?"

She nodded.

"Why?"

For several seconds she remained silent. Then she said, "It was on account of Jasper."

"Your brother?"

"Yes. Jasper was coming to town. I wanted to get a room for him. The hotels were full. Arthur had to get this place in the rooming house. He registered his own name and took the key. We intended to let Jasper stay there, but when Jasper didn't show up—well, I guess Arthur went down there and took the room himself after he had to leave the hotel."

Mason said, "Now this is important. Did *you* ever go there?"

"You mean to that rooming house?"

"Yes."

"I went there at 4 o'clock in the morning."

Mason whistled, then after a moment said, "This was the thing Sheldon told you not to say anything about?"

She nodded her head in silent misery. "I feel like a heel about it, Mr. Mason."

"You stayed there with Sheldon?"

"No, no, not with Sheldon! I took a separate room. There were rooms that could be rented that way. The woman who ran the place put a sign on the counter and . . ."

126

"I know all about that," Mason said. "But tell me, why did you rent this room?"

"I . . . well, Arthur got word to me that he had to see me."

"Gave you that address?"

"Yes."

"And what happened?"

"Arthur told me that when he got to the room he found something in it."

"You mean someone was there?"

"No. Something."

"A body."

"No, no. It was something else. Something terrible."

"What?"

"One of my fans."

"What about it?"

"It had been literally soaked in blood. It was—it was terrible."

"And Arthur said he found that in the room when he got there?"

"Yes."

"What did you do?"

"I took a room in the same rooming house and I worked over that fan, washing it in the washbowl and getting some of the worst of the stains out of it."

"Then what happened?"

"I threw the fan away."

"Where?"

"A place where it'll never be found."

Mason said, "There isn't any such place."

"Oh yes there is. I took it way out of town—way out on the outskirts and buried it."

"Where?"

"In a field."

"By the main highway?"

"No, I turned off on a side road and went up until I found a field. I dug a little hole with a shovel I had in the car—a small garden shovel—and buried the fan, and that's all there is to it."

"What time was it?"

"Just around daylight."

"Did Arthur go with you?"

"No."

"Did Arthur have any idea how the blood had got on the fan?"

"No."

"Or how the fan had got in his room?"

"No."

Mason studied her in frowning concentration for half a minute. "Do you," he asked, "know what happens to little girls who lie to their lawyers?"

"What?"

"In murder cases," Mason said, "they wind up in the death row at San Quentin, or perhaps because they're nice-looking women they get sent to prison for a term of years. How would you like to take ten years in the Women's Prison at Tehachapi? Ten years of prison. That would be nice, wouldn't it? Ten long years right out of your life, cooped up in a cell with no make-up, the clanging of iron doors, the drab routine of an eventless life. You . . ."

"Stop!" she screamed at him. "Stop! My God, what are you trying to do—pull my nerves out by the roots?"

"I'm trying to get you to tell the truth."

"I've told you the truth."

Mason said, "You've got to buck up. You've got to learn to face things. Right now you're going to get in the car with me and go to the police. You'd just heard they wanted to question you."

"But, Mr. Mason," she said in panic. "I thought you were keeping me here, keeping me hidden so that I . . ."

"Keeping you hidden long enough for the police to pick up a red herring that I threw across their trail," Mason said.

"But now you mean that I . . ."

"Exactly," Mason said. "The police are on the trail of the horse. They'll be here any time now."

"How bad is the case against me?"

"Either you're lying to me, or Sheldon lied to you, and you're pretty dumb to have let him tell you a story like that

128

and get away with it. In any event, the case against you is so black right now that I can't take a chance on having it made any blacker. You can't be in concealment. You can't be running away. You've got to go to the police. You'll have to talk; but be damn certain they don't trap you in any lies. Tell your story up to the time you left Callender at two o'clock, then deny everything, and clam up.''

"There's no other way out? Nothing else for me to do?''
"No.''
"All right," she said. "You wait here. I'll get my coat and hat and make up my face.''
"Your face looks all right now," Mason said.
"No, I'll . . . I'll be with you in a minute.''
She walked over to the bathroom, closed the door and called out, "You'll find a morning paper on the table, Mr. Mason.''

Mason picked up the paper from the table, settled back in the chair and after a quick glance at the headlines, read the comics and then turned to the sporting section. He read the baseball news, glanced at the financial section, then at his wristwatch, and called out, "Hey, make it snappy, Lois.''

There was no answer from the bathroom.

Mason moved over, knocked on the bathroom door. There was still no answer.

Mason jerked the door open.

The room was empty. The window at the far end was open and the screen had been taken off. In the soft ground outside of the window two heels had left an imprint in the soil.

The lawyer walked back to the other room, picked up his hat, carefully closed the door behind him, and walked toward the place where he had left his car.

The car was gone.

It was a good half mile before Mason came to a gas station that had a telephone. He called his office. "Hello, Della," he said. "How would you like to borrow a car from Paul Drake and come and get me?''

"Where are you?''

Mason gave her the address.

"What happened to your car?''

"It was stolen."

"Where's your client?"

"As far as I know, she's in my car."

"I'll be right out," Della told him cheerfully. "Hold everything."

Are you going to tell Della about it?...

Chapter 16

Della Street regarded Mason with twinkling eyes. She opened the door on the driver's side of Paul Drake's car and slid over so that Mason could get in behind the wheel.

"Painful?" she asked.

"Mentally painful," Mason said. "Damn it, that's what comes of getting sympathetic with women."

"Did you have to try to hide her in the first place?"

"I thought I did," Mason said. "I was trying to give her the breaks. I thought that if Sergeant Dorset got hold of Irene Kilby first, he'd bring in the witnesses to identify her. I thought there was a pretty good chance the witnesses might fall for it and identify . . . Oh well, it's all water under the bridge now."

"What are you going to do?"

"Do!" Mason said, indignantly. "I'm going to tell Lois Fenton to get herself a lawyer. I'm finished!"

"How did she do it, Chief?"

"Went into the bathroom, crawled out through the window. I'd left the keys in my car and she drove it away."

"Didn't you think she might do something like that?"

"Hell no. Why should she? I was sticking my neck out for her and telling her what had to be done. If she didn't like my advice all she had to do was say so. If she intended to run away, she could have walked right out of the front door. She acted as though *I* was trying to make the pinch."

"Is she guilty, Chief?"

Mason started to say something, then changed his mind and kept quiet.

Della asked, after a few moments, "What are you going to do about the car, report it as stolen?"

"No. I'm not going to do that to her. I'll give her that

much of a break. She'll probably get in touch with me some-time later in the day to tell me that my car is up in Oxnard or Ventura, or Santa Barbara, or Bakersfield, or somewhere, and I'll tell her she's got some money on deposit with me with which to hire another attorney.''

"Are you going to tell Paul Drake about her stealing the car?''

Mason said, "I don't tell anyone anything. Just tell Paul Drake I'm off the case. Tell him to call in his men. Then let it go at that. I'm going to a Turkish bath. Tell Paul his car is back and thanks.''

"Shall I tell him where you are?''

Mason shook his head, said, "Tell him to call his men off. To hell with it.''

He stopped the car in front of his club, climbed out and watched Della Street slide over behind the steering wheel. There was a twinkle in her eyes.

"I know,'' Mason said, grinning. "It's funny. I'll see the funny side of it myself when I come back to the office along toward five o'clock. Until then, you're the only one who thinks it's a joke. Bye-bye.''

She blew him a kiss.

Mason pounded his way across the sidewalk, entered the club, said to the doorman, "Why in hell is it that when a man has been victimized by a woman, every other woman he knows starts getting affectionate?''

"I wouldn't know, sir,'' the doorman said.

"No man would,'' Mason told him. "I guess it's just be-cause they are mentally putting the guy on a sucker list.''

"You may have something there, sir.''

"I may at that,'' Mason said, as he stepped into the elevator.

Two hours later Mason was dozing in the relaxed tran-quillity which follows a good Turkish bath and massage, when the attendant said, "Mr. Mason, you're wanted on the telephone. It's your secretary, and she says it's important.''

Mason roused himself from the relaxation of half-slumber, slippered his way across to the telephone, heard Della Street's voice, crisp with excitement, "Seen the afternoon paper, Chief?"

"No."

"It's just out. You'd better get one and then get over to the office."

"What's it about?" Mason asked.

"I'll read you the headlines," Della Street said. *"Murder Suspect Apprehended Escaping in Lawyer's Automobile—Attorney May Be Charged as Accomplice—Suspect Identified by Witnesses as Last Person to See Callender Alive . . ."*

"That's enough, Della. You can stop right there. I'm coming over."

Chapter 17

Mason, Della Street, and Paul Drake sat in a grim conference long after office hours.

"They've got a dead open and shut airtight case against her," Drake said, "and the D.A. is going to move in on you if you don't reach an agreement with him."

"What sort of an agreement?"

"They'll let her cop a plea."

"Manslaughter?"

"I think they're going to hold out for second degree."

"What else?"

Drake said, "They've got evidence to burn. It's the only thing to do, Perry."

"Just how much evidence have they got, Paul?"

"Scads of it, Perry. The witnesses identify her as the woman who went into the hotel room around twenty minutes past two. The house detective can swear that Callender was alive at that time because he himself put through the telephone call to Callender's room, heard Callender say hello, and then turned the phone over to the fan-dancer.

"She had motive to burn. She was trying to protect her brother. The police have located the brother. He's a sap. He gave them a signed statement. He's just one of those things and he sobbed out his whole story to the police. He worked at one time for John Callender. He embezzled some money and he forged two cheques. Just a weak kid playing the races."

"I know that already," Mason said.

"Here's what you don't know. When Callender started to put the bite on Lois the second time, Fenton got all hopped up on a couple of marijuana cigarettes and decided he'd get into Callender's house and burglarize the safe and recover the evidence. He had the combination to the safe, because he'd worked there. Young Fenton knew that he couldn't get past the dogs and the watchman unless he resorted to some subterfuge, so he hit on the expedient of borrowing his sister's horse and riding up to the ranch at night. Callender's quite a horseman and he had a few guests there who do a bit of riding, so it wouldn't attract any great amount of attention if a man came riding up on horseback. Anyway, that's what young Fenton thought.''

''All right,'' Mason said, ''so he tried to steal the papers. I take it he didn't do it?''

''He didn't do it. The watchman spotted him, yelled at him to stop, and took a shot at him. It was a close call. The shot grazed the horse's back and lodged in the saddle.''

''Fenton has confessed to all that?''

''Wait a minute, you haven't heard anything yet.''

''Go ahead.''

''Then Fenton got in a panic. He was afraid to take the horse back to his sister's place because he realized that bullet in the saddle constituted evidence, so he rode the horse in the other direction for a while, then turned him loose and hitchhiked back to Brawley.''

''Nice smart boy, wasn't he?''

''Oh, smart as hell.''

''What's the rest of it?''

''Callender sent for Jasper Fenton to come to see him at the Richmell.''

''What time?''

''The kid was to be there promptly at two. He didn't make it because he needed a few drinks first. He showed up forty-five minutes late. He opened the door, saw Callender's body on the floor and beat it. He was too scared to notify the officers until the next day. He's a weak sister, a drip. Faulkner identifies him as the man who popped in to Callender's room and then popped right out again.''

''Could the kid have killed Callender, Paul?''

''Hell, Perry, he wasn't in there long enough. If we hadn't had that operative watching the corridor, he would have been a cinch. The police would have pinned it on him and the kid

135

never would have been able to talk his way out of it. But he wasn't in there ten seconds altogether."

Mason said, "It doesn't take long to stick a sword in a man."

"No, but it takes a while to find the weapon, if you haven't got one. One thing is certain, he wasn't carrying a Japanese sword with him and he couldn't have gone into Callender's room, walked past Callender, found a weapon which was lying opportunely near by, and pushed it into Callender's chest. It was Callender's sword. Callender brought it with him when he came to the hotel."

"So what do the police say?"

"The obvious thing, Perry, it's mathematical. Lois Fenton was trying to protect her brother. She had tried marrying Callender and living with him. She knew that wasn't going to work. She'd rather do anything than go through with that again. All right, she goes to see Callender. Callender has probably pulled all the old threats. He's going to prosecute first thing in the morning, and all that sort of stuff. But in the back of Lois Fenton's mind an idea is germinating. When she was in the room she saw this Japanese sword of Callender's lying on the table. She . . ."

"Wait a minute," Mason interrupted. "You're sure it's Callender's sword?"

"It's Callender's sword. He brought it in with him from his ranch. A Japanese sword that he evidently intended to trade off, or have fixed, or something. Anyway, he brought it in from his ranch. The doorman remembers it. The bellboy who checked him in at the hotel remembers that he had it when he came in. It was his sword. It was in his room lying on the table."

"How about your shadowing jobs, did they lead anywhere?"

Drake said, "Nothing that'll help. Sheldon left that rooming house, took a bus to San Diego and then chartered a plane for Nogales. My man didn't want to go to the expense of a plane so he phoned me and I got a man from Tucson to go on down and be there when the plane arrived. But Sheldon had taken a powder. When his chartered plane stopped for gas he got out to wander around the airport. No one saw him after that. He left his coat and suitcase in the plane. It was, of course, reported to the police and they're hunting him."

"What about the girl, this Cherie Chi-Chi?"

"She was a cinch. I got a man who picked up her trail just as she was leaving thē building. She went to her apartment, stayed for a while, then to the office of Barlow, the booking agent. Sergeant Dorset picked her up there and they went away fast, using the siren. My man couldn't keep up so he quit. Apparently Dorset took her to the D.A., or to head-quarters. She made her story stand up so they turned her loose—but she isn't back at her apartment yet. I'm keeping it covered to pick her up when she comes back."

"All right," Mason said, "it still isn't open and shut against anybody."

"Oh, yes, it is, Perry. Remember that when Lois Fenton came into the hotel at 2.23 the house dick stopped her. She told him she was going up to see Callender. He made her telephone Callender and get an okay. There you have it in a nutshell. Callender was alive at 2.23. He was dead at 2.44. There was only one person who was in the room between 2.23 and 2.44, and that was your client, Lois Fenton, and she was in there long enough to have had an argument with him, to have picked up the sword and pushed it through his chest, and there you are."

"They've identified her?" Mason asked.

Drake nodded.

"They didn't identify the other fan-dancer?"

"Don't be silly, Perry. Lieutenant Tragg is a damn smart cookie. I don't know what happened when Sergeant Dorset picked up this Cherie Chi-Chi. I don't know what she told him, but I do know that the person that was identified by the witnesses was Lois Fenton. I do know that it's Lois Fenton who is being charged with first-degree murder."

"Any fingerprints on the sword?" Mason asked.

"No fingerprints on the sword. She had enough presence of mind to wipe the hilt. I tell you, Perry, you've got to take a plea. You can't beat it."

"How about Sheldon?"

137

"Callender was alive after Sheldon left Callender's room."

"How did Sheldon know he was dead when he put the DO NOT DISTURB sign on the door?"

"The murder must have been premeditated, Perry. Sheldon couldn't have known it otherwise. He must have known Lois was planning to do it. There were no phone calls to or from his room after 1.30. The night switchboard operators swear to that. You going to plead her to second degree, Perry?"

"Not unless she wants to plead," Mason said grimly. "She's my client now. Catching her escaping in my car ties me right in with her. I'm stuck with her, but as long as she's my client I'll play it her way."

"Couldn't you tell Tragg she stole the car, Perry?"

Mason laughed without humour. After a moment Paul Drake said, "Yes, I see your point, Perry."

Mason got to his feet. "All right, I'm stuck with her. Let's go, Paul."

Chapter 18

The courtroom was stilled with an electric tension. There was that degree of silence which made even the sound of a cough seem magnified out of all proportion.

Judge Donahue said, "Gentlemen, the defendant is in court. A jury has been selected and sworn to try the case. The District Attorney has made his opening statement to the jury. Does the defence wish to make its opening statement at this time?"

Mason said, "No, your honour, we will reserve our opening statement until we start putting on our defence."

"Very well. The District Attorney will call his first witness."

"Doctor Jackson Lambert," Burger announced.

Doctor Lambert took the stand.

Mason said, "Subject to the right of cross-examination, we will stipulate to Doctor Lambert's professional qualifications."

"Very well," Burger said. "Doctor Lambert, did you perform a post-mortem upon the body of John Callender?"

"I did. Yes, sir."

"At the time that you first saw that body, will you please explain the position and condition of the body and what you observed, if anything?"

"The body was lying partially on its right side," Doctor Lambert said. "A sword had been pushed entirely through the body of the decedent so that some four and a half inches of the blade protruded on the other side of the body, that is, through the back. The blade had been driven in through the chest. I am talking now about what I discovered when I first saw the body."

"Go on, Doctor."

"Subsequently, I performed a post-mortem upon the body. I determined that the cause of death was the blade which had been driven through the body. I fixed the time of death as approximately between 1.30 and 3.00 o'clock on the morning of September seventeenth, determining the time of death from the temperature of the body, the temperature of the room, the lapse rate of temperature, and several other factors."

"Now, Doctor, did you find any foreign substance in the body near the wound, or within the chest wall?"

"I did."

"What?"

"I found portions of a feather. Perhaps I may be permitted to explain. A feather consists of various parts. There is a central shaft, the proximal part of which is hollow and which is termed the quill. There are processes on each side of this quill which are called barbs. These barbs, in turn, have barbules, which in turn have barbicels. Microscopically these have hooks, which in turn interlock with other barbules and barbicels so as to give the feather a certain cohesive integrity.

"Now then, in the post-mortem I found portions of the barbs of two ostrich plumes, together with fragmentary barbules and barbicels, sufficient in quantity to be identified as portions of an ostrich plume."

"You have those particles with you, Doctor?"

"I have, yes, sir."

"How did you preserve them, Doctor?"

"In a test tube, floating in alcohol."

The Doctor took a small glass tube from his pocket and handed it to the district attorney.

"And these are the feathers, or the portions of the feather, which you recovered from the body of the decedent?"

"That is right."

"We request that this be introduced in evidence as People's Exhibit Number 1," Burger asked.

"Any objection?" Judge Donahue asked Mason.

"No objection, your Honour."

"Anything else that you noticed, Doctor?"

"The hands of the decedent," the doctor said, "were

140

clutched about the razor-keen blade of the sword. The edge had cut deep into the fingers of both hands. One eye was partially open; one was closed. The body was fully clothed. There had been some rather extensive external hæmorrhage through the back and there had been a very extensive internal hæmorrhage.''

"Death was instantaneous?''

"Practically instantaneous.''

"You may inquire,'' Burger said.

Mason shook his head with an appearance of the greatest indifference. "No questions,'' he said. "I think the doctor's testimony undoubtedly covers the situation as he saw it.''

Hamilton Burger was plainly surprised. "No cross-examination?'' he asked.

"No cross-examination,'' Mason said, smiling, his tone indicating that after all the presence of the portions of an ostrich plume in the body was of no particular importance.

"Your Honour,'' Hamilton Burger said, "there is a portion of the proof which I would like to put on at this time so as to connect up this evidence of Doctor Lambert. I think perhaps that I will be departing from the conventional order of proof, and yet I wish to have this other evidence presented now because I wish to ask Doctor Lambert some more questions in connection with that evidence; therefore, I wish to go ahead with this phase of the case now.''

"It's your case,'' Judge Donahue said. "Go ahead and put it on any way you wish. I don't know as there is any rule of law concerning the order of proof, except that if objection is made it is necessary to prove the *corpus delicti* before other aspects of the case can be introduced, and even in such case, in the absence of objection, proof can be received and connected up later.''

"Very well. I wish to call Freeman Gurley.''

Freeman Gurley, attired in overalls and jumper, walked to the witness stand with the long, easy stride of an outdoor man.

Gurley quickly answered the usual preliminary questions as to his name, occupation and residence. He was, he explained, somewhat unnecessarily in view of his wearing apparel, a farmer.

"Now then," Hamilton Burger went on, triumphantly, "have you ever seen this defendant before, the young woman sitting there just in back of her counsel and to the right of the deputy sheriff?"

"Yes, sir, I saw her before."

"When?"

"On the morning of September seventeenth."

"Where was she?"

"She was at the south-east end of my ranch."

"Now, I would like to identify your ranch a little more closely. I have here a map which I will authenticate later, but in the meantime, simply as a diagram, I wish to ask you certain questions about it."

"Yes, sir."

Burger unrolled a map.

"Do you recognize the lines on this map; that is, do you recognize what it purports to show?"

"Yes, sir."

"What does it show?"

"It shows the general location of my ranch. The house is marked on the map, and the road and fence are marked, and the position of the barn is marked; also the shade trees and the position of a corral near the barn."

"And this purports to show the ranch on which you were living on the morning of September seventeenth?"

"That's right."

"And does this map appear to be correct?"

"It does. Yes, sir."

"Now you say you saw the defendant at the time mentioned?"

"Yes, sir."

"What did she do?"

"She drove along this road in a car."

"Let's have the map hung on the blackboard," Hamilton Burger said, "and you can step over to it and identify the places on the map as you talk. Now just go ahead."

The map was hung up and Gurley said, "She stopped her car right about here."

"All right, just indicate that point on the map."

"She got out and looked around and then she opened the door on the left-hand side of the car and took out a shovel."

"And then what did she do?"

"Then she took something else out of the car. I couldn't see what it was. It was some sort of a black object, some sort of a case."

"About the size and shape of a violin case?" Burger asked.

"Objected to as leading and suggestive. If the Court please, let this witness tell what he saw, not what the District Attorney would like to have had him see."

"Objection is sustained," Judge Donahue said, "and the Court will call attention of counsel to the fact that the vice of a leading question consists in having asked it. Sustaining an objection to a leading question really does no good, because the idea has already been implanted in the mind of the witness. Counsel will please refrain from asking leading questions except on cross-examination, or at such time as leading questions are permitted. Now proceed with the examination, Mr. Burger."

"I'm sorry, your Honour," Burger said. "Can you describe this black object, Mr. Gurley?"

"Well, it was sort of a case of some sort. Something like a gun case, only it wasn't. It was black and different shaped from a gun case."

"Very well. What happened?"

"This young woman put these things over the fence and then—and then, well, she just pulled her skirts—way up."

"And what did she do then?"

"She climbed up over the barbed-wire fence."

"What do you mean when you say she climbed the fence?"

"She put one of her hands on the top of a wooden post and climbed up the strands of barbed wire just like it was a ladder. Then when she got to the top she put one foot on the top strand of barbed wire and vaulted over to the ground on the other side."

"Then what did she do?"

"Then she picked up this case and the shovel, she went over and dug a hole, took something out of the case, put it in the hole, covered it up and then went back to the car."

"Then what?"

"She put the shovel and the case in the car, got in the car and drove away."

"And what did you do?"

"I waited until she had gone and then I went down to the place where she had been digging and dug up what she had buried."

"And what did you find?"

"An ostrich-plume fan that had been soaked in blood and . . ."

"Just a minute, just a minute," Hamilton Burger said. "Don't testify as an expert, Mr. Gurley. You don't know that the fan had been soaked in blood. That's a matter for the doctors to testify to. Just tell us what *you found*."

"Well, I found a fan."

"And what did you do with it?"

"I rang up the sheriff's office and told them what I had found, and the sheriff came out with some man and picked up the fan."

"That man was Lieutenant Tragg of the metropolitan Homicide Squad?"

"I believe it was, yes, sir. He was introduced to me as Lieutenant Tragg."

"Would you know that fan if you saw it again?"

"Yes, sir."

"Did you do anything to this fan before you turned it over to Lieutenant Tragg and the sheriff?"

"Do anything to it? No."

"I mean, did you do anything so you could identify it?

"Oh, yes, at the suggestion of Lieutenant Tragg I wrote my initials on it."

With something of a flourish, Hamilton Burger reached under the counsel table, took out a long suitcase, opened it, took out a fan and handed it to the witness. "Have you ever seen this fan before?"

"Yes, sir, that is the fan I dug up. My initials are on it."

Burger said, "Your Honour, I will connect this fan up later. At the moment I wish it marked for identification as People's Exhibit Number 2."

He turned to Perry Mason and snapped, "Cross-examine!"

Mason walked over to the map, said, "Let me get the scale of this map. Oh, yes—now let's see . . . Let's measure this . . . Oh, yes, it seems to be some one thousand feet from your house to this place where the fan was buried. Is that right?"

"About three hundred yards, I would say."

"And do you mean to say that you recognized this defendant from a distance of three hundred yards?"

Hamilton Burger turned to the jury and let the jurors see the broad, triumphant grin which now suffused his countenance.

"Yes, sir," the witness said.

"Are your eyes any better than the average?" Mason asked. "Do you have better vision, better eyesight?"

"I don't think so. No."

"Then how did you recognize the defendant at that distance?"

"With the aid of a pair of seven-power binoculars," the witness said.

Hamilton Burger threw back his head and chuckled audibly.

Mason showed no discomfiture. "Exactly," he said, as though he had been expecting such an answer. "You had binoculars. Now this episode took place early in the morning?"

"Yes, sir."

"The sun was up?"

"Well, the sun was just . . . Well, I won't say that the sun *was* up."

"It may have been before sun-up?"

"Yes."

"And the magnification of the binoculars was seven power?"

"That's right. Seven by fifties they were. The way I figure that out, that gives me a magnification of seven diameters.

145

We'll say that it's a thousand feet in round figures. That gives me the same kind of view that I'd have at about a hundred and forty-some feet."

"Provided the conditions of visibility were perfect and not taking into consideration the amount of light which is absorbed by the binocular lenses themselves," Mason pointed out.

"Well, anyway, I could see her plain enough to recognize her. I saw her just as plain as day."

"And you watched her burying the fan?"

"That's right."

Burger's grin was visible now to those in the courthouse as he swung about in his swivel-chair, quite evidently enjoying this cross-examination.

"You were up, getting ready to do your farm work?" Mason asked.

"That's right."

"And where were you, in the kitchen or in the . . ."

"In the kitchen."

"You'd finished breakfast or were just eating breakfast?"

"Just finishing up."

"You're a married man?"

"Yes, sir."

"And your wife was there in the kitchen?"

"Yes, sir."

"Now do you want this jury to understand," Mason asked, accusingly, "that during all of this time when you were looking at these goings on through the binoculars, your wife didn't ask to take the binoculars or that you were so selfish you didn't let her see anything of what was going on?"

"Well . . ." The witness hesitated. "Yes, she had them part of the time."

"How much of the time?"

"Well, she took them after we saw the girl get over the fence."

"Oh, yes," Mason said, "and did she give them back to you?"

"Yes."

"When?"

"After a few seconds."

"You saw the girl get over the fence?"

"That's right."

"And then your wife took the binoculars?"

"Yes, sir."

"And who had the binoculars while the girl was digging the hole?"

"The wife did."

"Who had the binoculars while the girl was opening the case?"

"The wife did."

"Who had the binoculars while the girl was putting something which she took out of the black case into the hole she had dug?"

"The missus."

"Who had the binoculars while the girl was covering up the hole?"

"The missus."

"Who had the binoculars when the girl started toward the fence?"

"I did."

"Who had the binoculars when the girl pulled up her skirts and got over the fence the second time?"

"The wife."

"Who had the binoculars when the girl got in the car and drove away?"

"I did."

"Then how," Mason said, "can you tell what the girl was doing while she was putting something in this hole? How can you tell where she got the thing that she took from the black case . . ."

"All the time the wife had the binoculars she kept on telling me what she was seeing through them."

"So what you are now testifying to is predicated on what your wife told you?"

"Sure."

There was no longer any smile on Hamilton Burger's face.

"I move to strike out all parts of this witness's testimony relating to the young woman taking an object from the case

147

and putting it in the hole that had been dug in the ground, because it now appears that evidence is hearsay," Mason said.

Judge Donahue pursed his lips. "I'm afraid the Court is going to have to grant the motion, Mr. Burger."

"Just a moment," Burger said desperately. "May I ask a few questions on redirect examination?"

"In order to try and clarify the situation as it now exists?"

"Yes, your Honour."

"Apparently, Mr. Burger," Judge Donahue said, "the motion of the defendant as the evidence now stands is well taken. The portions of the testimony that counsel has moved to strike out are plainly hearsay testimony. That motion will be granted. Now you have the right, on redirect examination, to bring out any additional facts you can or facts by way of explanation."

"Very well, your Honour," Hamilton Burger said, savagely, making no attempt to conceal his displeasure at the turn of events. "Mr. Gurley, all the time that your wife had the binoculars, what were you doing?"

"I was standing right beside her, listening to what she said."

"Never mind anything about listening to your wife," Burger snapped. "Tell me where you were standing."

"Right behind her."

"And she was at a window?"

"Yes."

"Then you could look through the window and see what was taking place?"

"Yes."

"Then you, yourself, saw this young woman . . ."

"Just a moment," Mason interrupted. "We're getting into leading questions again."

"That's right," Judge Donahue said. "I feel that it would be very prejudicial to have counsel lead the witness at this point."

"All right," Burger snapped, "what did you do?"

"I looked out of the window."

"What did you see?"

"I saw what was going on."

"Then you weren't testifying to hearsay evidence at all," Burger said. "You were testifying to what you saw, is that right?"

"That's right."

"Then you saw her . . ."

"Kindly don't lead the witness," Judge Donahue said curtly.

"Well, what *did* you see?"

"Well, I saw her do everything I've described."

"Now cross-examine again, if you wish," Burger shot out at Mason.

"You were standing behind your wife?" Mason asked.

"That's right."

"Looking over your wife's head?"

"Yes."

Mason said, "Now at those times when you did not have the binoculars, you were watching this young woman do certain things at a distance of something over a thousand feet."

"Well, I put it around nine hundred feet, around three hundred yards."

"Let's scale it on the map and find out how far it is," Mason said.

He took a rule from his pocket, scaled off the distance and said, "I make it one thousand and forty-two feet."

"I didn't think it was that far."

"The map says it's that far," Mason said, "and you've already testified the map is correct. I take it that the map is correct. Let's assume that is was one thousand and forty-two feet, at any rate, over a thousand feet. Now you were looking at what was going on before daylight at a distance of over one thousand feet?"

"Yes."

"Now," Mason said, "when your wife was looking through the binoculars, she had raised the window?"

"She didn't raise the window, I did."

"Exactly," Mason said. "In using binoculars, you get a distorted view if you look through plain window glass, do you not?"

"Yes. And the glass was pretty dusty. We'd had rain and wind and the missus hadn't got around to washing windows."

"So you raised the lower pane of the window?"

"That's right."

"And when you were looking over your wife's shoulders you were considerably higher than she was?" Mason asked.

"Yes."

"And your wife was sitting in a chair by the open window?"

"That's right."

"Steadying the binoculars by resting her elbows on the window sill?"

"Yes."

"Then you must have been looking out through the *upper* part of the window."

"I was."

"But if you had raised the window," Mason said, "then the lower part of the window was raised so that it was adjacent to the upper part of the window, so that you were then looking through two thicknesses of window glass."

"Yes, I guess I was."

"And do you want the jury to understand that you now claim that you could identify the defendant and follow her every move while you were watching her through two thicknesses of dirty, dusty windowpane glass before it was broad daylight at a distance of one thousand and forty-two feet?"

The witness squirmed. "Well, I had already seen her through the binoculars."

"That's right, but as far as the rest of it is concerned, you don't know who it was who was out there, do you?"

"Well, it must have been the same person that I saw through the binoculars."

"But you can't swear that it was the same person."

"Well, no, I can't swear to it."

"That's all," Mason said.

"But you do *know* that it must have been the same person," Burger shouted.

"Tut, tut," Mason said. "There we go with those leading questions again."

"Well, it's a foregone conclusion," Burger said, irritably. "The witness knows no one else took her place and . . . It's purely a mathematical conclusion, your Honour."

"Let it stay a mathematical conclusion then," Judge Donahue said. "You're coming dangerously close to the border line, Counsellor."

"Yes, your Honour. I'm sorry."

"Try and be more careful. Call your next witness."

"I want Doctor Jackson Lambert to take the stand again for a few questions," Burger said, his face still flushed with anger.

Doctor Lambert returned to the stand.

"Calling your attention to this fan which has been identified by the witness Gurley, whose testimony I take it you heard, Doctor?"

"Yes, sir."

"I ask you if you have previously seen this fan."

"I have, yes, sir."

"And you made some study of it?"

"I have, yes, sir."

"What sort of a study?"

"A microscopic examination of the feathers and all of the various parts. A chemical examination for human blood-stains."

"Now, Doctor, I want you to hold the fan partially open and in front of you, so that it screens your eyes. Now, Doctor, when you have done this, near the base of the fan do you observe any distinguishing mark?"

"I do, yes, sir."

"What is that mark?"

"There is a wedge-shaped cut in one of the quills."

"Is that cut such as would have been made in the event a sharp sword of the dimensions of the sword which you found in the body of the decedent had been thrust through the fan at that point?"

"Objected to," Mason said, "on the ground that the question is argumentative, that it calls for a conclusion of the

151

witness upon a subject which is not proper medical examination, or properly the subject for an expert witness. It is one of the questions which the jurors will be called on to decide after the evidence is in. It is an attempt to interpret evidence rather than to reach a subject within the legitimate province of expert or medical opinion."

"Sustained," Judge Donahue said.

"Very well," Burger said with some exasperation. "I will now call your attention, Doctor, to the feathery projections coming out from this quill, and I will ask you if you have made a microscopic examination of the bits of feather in the test tube which has been introduced as People's Exhibit Number 1, and the corresponding portions of feather which are adjacent to this V-shaped cut in the quill."

"I have, yes, sir."

"What did you find?"

"I found that so far as could be ascertained, they were absolutely identical in colour, context and composition."

"What are the slightly reddish brown stains on this fan, Doctor?"

"Those are blood stains."

"What sort of blood, Doctor?"

"Human blood."

"Cross-examine," Burger snapped at Mason.

"You say that the bits of feather which you recovered from the body of the decedent were exactly the same in three particulars, Doctor?"

"That's right."

"What were those particulars?"

"Colour, context and composition."

"That sounds rather formidable, Doctor," Mason observed conversationally. "Now as to colour, the colour, I believe, is white."

"That's right."

"Did you ever see an ostrich-plume fan used by a fandancer which wasn't white?"

"Well, no."

"All right," Mason said. "Then, so far as colour is concerned, the colour was exactly the same as that of every other
152

fan you have ever seen used by any fan-dancer. Is that correct?"

"That's right, I guess."

"Now, as far as context is concerned, what do you mean by that?"

"Well, I mean it was of the same substance as this feather on this fan."

"And, by the same sign, the same context as any other ostrich plume. You didn't try to differentiate between ostrich plumes, did you?"

"No."

"Did you compare these bits of feather, which you recovered from the wound, with any other ostrich plume?"

"No, sir."

"Only with ostrich plumes from this fan?"

"That's right."

"So in short, Doctor, while your testimony on these three particulars sounds rather convincing when you use the technical terms, the fact remains that what you mean is that this fan is composed of ostrich feathers; that the bits of feather you found in the body of the decedent came, in your opinion, from an ostrich plume, and that's all you know, is that right?"

"Well . . . well, if you want to put it that way, I guess that's about the size of it."

"In other words, for all you know those bits of feather could have come from any other ostrich plume in the world?"

"Well, of course, there's this cut in the quill of this fan which could have been made . . ."

"Could have been made by any kind of knife at any time, isn't that right, Doctor?"

"Well, it was made by a sharp knife and the indications are that it was a blade that tapered at a certain angle."

"You don't know with what type of blade that was made?"

"Well, of course you can guess . . ."

"Exactly, Doctor, and we don't want guesswork. We want facts. There's only a cut in that quill. It isn't a section that has been removed, therefore you have no way of knowing the exact slope of the sides of the blade."

"Well, I guess not."

"Therefore, that cut could have been made by any knife?"

"Well—well, yes, I guess so."

"There's nothing to indicate the time at which the cut was made?"

"No, sir."

"So this cut could have been made at any time by any knife?"

"Yes, sir."

"And the bits of feather which you found in the body of the decedent could have come from any ostrich plume. Is that right?"

"Put it that way if you want to."

"I've already put it that way. Answer the question. Is that right?"

"Yes, that's right," the Doctor said, thoroughly exasperated.

"And that's all," Mason said, smiling at the jury.

And it was significant that two or three of the jurors unashamedly smiled back.

Quite apparently Hamilton Burger had intended to build up his case in such a way that the jurors would be prejudiced against the defendant right at the start of the case. Now that this attempt had failed to accomplish its purpose, the District Attorney fell back upon the routine procedure. He proved the identity of the dead body, he introduced photographs showing the body as it had been found in the hotel room. Then, once more, he built to a dramatic climax as the clock showed it was approaching the hour of adjournment.

"Call Samuel Meeker," he said.

Samuel Meeker took the stand, gave his full name, his age, residence, and his occupation as being that of a hotel employee.

"In what capacity are you employed by the hotel?" the District Attorney asked.

"House detective, sir."

"What hotel?"

"The Richmell Hotel."

"That was the hotel where the body of John Callender was found?"

"Yes, sir."

"Now were you so employed as house detective on September the sixteenth and seventeenth?"

"I was, yes, sir."

"Directing your attention particularly to events which transpired early in the morning of the seventeenth. Can you tell us anything of what happened?"

"Yes, sir."

"What happened?"

"Well, at twenty minutes past two in the morning this young woman appeared in the lobby of the hotel."

"Now when you say 'this young woman' who do you mean?"

"The young woman sitting there."

"You are pointing at the defendant, Lois Fenton?"

"That's right. Yes, sir."

"Then she is the one you mean when you say that 'this young woman appeared in the lobby of the hotel'?"

"Yes, sir, that's right."

"And what did she do?"

"She started toward the elevators."

"And what happened?"

"I spoke to her and asked her if she had a room in the hotel and she said she didn't, but that she wanted to see someone who did have a room in the hotel. In view of the fact that it was an exceedingly late and unusual hour for a woman to be paying a call on any person who had a room in the hotel, I insisted that she tell me the name of the party."

"Did she?"

"Yes, sir."

"And what did she say?"

"She said it was John Callender."

"And what did you do?"

"I asked her if John Callender was expecting her, and she said he was, so then I insisted that she accompany me over to the house telephones and I picked up the receiver and asked for Mr. Callender's room."

"What happened?"

"After a moment, Mr. Callender said hello, and I immediately handed the telephone over to this young lady."

"Now let's have one thing definitely understood," Burger said. "Whenever you mention 'this young woman,' to whom are you referring?"

"To the defendant, Lois Fenton, sitting there."

"All right, you refer to the defendant here, Lois Fenton."

"That's right."

"Now, you handed her the receiver as soon as you heard John Callender answer the phone?"

"Yes, sir."

"And what happened?"

"Well, of course I could hear only one end of the conversation."

"I understand. Go on."

"Well, this young woman, that is Lois Fenton, the defendant there, said that she was in the lobby, that she had been having some trouble with a house detective who had stopped her and wanted to be sure that she had an appointment; that the house detective had been the one who had placed the call, and that she would be right up."

"You didn't hear what reply Callender made to that?"

"No. I just heard her make the statement that she'd be right up. Then she hung up the phone. Apparently it was all right. However, as far as I was concerned, she had been announced and that was all I cared about. You understand, Mr. Callender was sort of a privileged person around the hotel; that is, he could do things that transient tenants couldn't. You see, in a hotel of that sort we're anxious to make the guests comfortable, but we also want to be sure that there is nothing offensive to the other guests, particularly noisy parties and things like that. Well, Mr. Callender was always a very fine tenant as far as things of that sort were concerned. He was quite a nighthawk and would do business until late at night, having people come in to see him at all hours. Sometimes at two and three o'clock in the morning, sometimes even later, but he was always very discreet and never made any racket, and we never had any complaints."

156

"I gather that Mr. Callender kept a room there permanently?"

"Yes, sir. That's right."

"Now the defendant hung up the telephone and then what did she do?"

"Walked to the elevators and went up to the fifth floor."

"How do you know it was the fifth floor?"

"I watched the indicator to make certain that was where she got off."

"Was she carrying anything in her hand?"

"Yes, sir."

"What?"

"A black violin case."

"Did it seem to be heavy or light—from the way she was carrying it?"

"Objected to," Mason said. "The question, if your Honour please, calls for a conclusion of the witness and opinion evidence."

"Objection sustained."

"Do you know when she came down?"

"Yes."

"When?"

"At a little after 2.33. I happened to look at the clock as she came out."

"Now, did you have any unusual experiences on the fifth floor of that hotel during the early hours of the morning of September seventeenth?"

"Yes, sir, I did."

"What happened?"

"Around thirty-five minutes past two o'clock in the morning I went up to the fifth floor."

"Then that must have been within a minute or two after the defendant left?"

"It was, yes, sir."

"You went up to the fifth floor. For what purpose?"

"Objected to as incompetent, irrelevant and immaterial," Mason said.

"Sustained."

"Well, you *did* go up to the fifth floor?"

"Yes."

"And when you left the elevator," Burger said, his manner showing his exasperation, "did you turn toward John Callender's room or in the other direction?"

"I turned toward John Callender's room."

"And where did you go?"

"I didn't go only a few steps. I happened to notice that the door of the mop closet was partially ajar. I opened it and found a Mr. Faulkner in there. Mr. Faulkner told me that he was a . . ."

"Never mind what Mr. Faulkner told you. I just want to show by you that you found Mr. Faulkner there in the closet at that time."

"That's right, I did."

"Now, then, at any time during the morning did you change places with Mr. Faulkner; that is, did you enter the mop closet?"

"I did. Yes, sir."

"When was that?"

"That was at approximately three minutes past three o'clock in the morning."

"Why did you do that?"

"I did it to watch the corridor."

"Why were you watching the corridor?"

"Mr. Faulkner had been watching the corridor."

"Never mind about Mr. Faulkner. I'm asking *you* what *you* did."

"Yes, sir. At approximately three minutes past three o'clock in the morning, or perhaps four minutes past three o'clock in the morning, by the time I actually got off the elevator, I went up and took my place in the mop closet and started watching the corridor."

"What part of the corridor?"

"The corridor on the fifth floor which led to the room occupied by John Callender."

"Did you see anything? That is, did you see anyone go into or leave the room occupied by John Callender?"

"No, sir, I did not."

"You may cross-examine," Burger said.

"Are you absolutely positive that the woman you saw there in the lobby was this defendant?" Mason asked on cross-examination.

"Yes, sir. I am."

"You identified her at the police station?"

"Yes, sir."

"Where was she?"

"She was marched into what is known as a shadow box, with some five or six other women, all of them about the same age and about the same size and build."

"And you identified her?"

"Yes, sir, I identified her positively and absolutely at that time."

"And you have seen her since?"

"Several times, yes, sir."

"You've talked with her?"

"Yes, sir."

"You had never seen this young woman before that time she appeared in the lobby of the Richmell Hotel on the morning of the seventeenth?"

"Not to the best of my knowledge, no, sir."

"And you didn't see her again until after she was in police custody?"

"I saw her when she went out of the hotel."

"I understand. You saw her come in and you saw her go out, but you didn't see her again after that until you were called upon to identify her in that shadow box, is that right?"

"That's right."

"When was this?"

"On the eighteenth. The day after the murder."

"And you identified the defendant?"

"I did. Yes, sir."

"You're absolutely positive that there can be no mistake in your identification?"

"Positive, yes, sir."

"You wear glasses?"

"I do. Yes, sir."

"You had those glasses on on the morning of the seventeenth?"

"I did, yes, sir."

"And again on the eighteenth when you identified the defendant?"

"Yes, sir."

"No further cross-examination," Mason said.

"No further direct. That's all, Mr. Meeker," Burger said. "If the Court please, I believe I have time for one more witness. At least I can start with him."

"Very well, go ahead. We'll work right on until five o'clock," Judge Donahue said.

"Call Frank Faulkner," Burger snapped.

Frank Faulkner came forward, was sworn, testified to his name and to his occupation, the fact that he was acquainted with Perry Mason, that he was employed by the Drake Detective Agency and that early on the morning of the seventeenth he had been instructed to proceed to the Richmell Hotel and establish himself in a position where he could observe the corridor; that he had arrived at the hotel on the morning of the seventeenth at approximately twenty minutes past two; that he had taken up his position in the mop closet and had no sooner established himself there when he saw a man emerge from room 511, which was occupied by John Callender, and rush across the hall to enter the room numbered 510, that being the room directly opposite; that at approximately two twenty-two and a half the defendant, Lois Fenton, had left the elevator, walked down the hall and gone into room 511; that she had been in there for just a little over nine minutes, leaving the room at 2.33, and getting in the elevator a few seconds later; that at 2.44 a man whom he did not know at the time, but whom he subsequently had learned was Jasper Fenton, left the elevator, entered room 511 and came out almost immediately, hurried back down the corridor to the elevator and went out; that at two minutes past three Arthur Sheldon, the occupant of room 510, had checked out and had gone down to the lobby; that pursuant to arrangements the witness had made with the house detective as soon as Arthur Sheldon checked out, the house detective came up to relieve the witness and the witness went down to the desk where he was able to secure room 510; that thereafter he

160

returned to room 510 and from that point of vantage kept watch on the room across the corridor; that no person went into that room or left that room until after he had been joined by another operative, at which time he had lain down on the bed.

He looked at Mason meaningly as he made this last statement, apparently trying to indicate to the lawyer that he had deliberately refrained from telling the police anything about Mason's visit to the room where the body had been found. The witness then went on to state that at about 5.30 A.M. Harvey Julian, the other detective in the employ of the Drake Detective Agency, had come to relieve him.

"And you are positive that the person whom you saw leaving the elevator at approximately two twenty-two and a half and going down to John Callender's room was this defendant, Lois Fenton?" Hamilton Burger asked.

"I am, yes, sir."

"And how about the person who subsequently emerged from that room and went down the corridor toward the elevator?"

"The same person."

"Was that person carrying anything?"

"Yes, sir."

"What?"

"A black violin case."

"At the time she walked down the corridor to the room?"

"Yes, sir."

"And at the time she came back?"

"Yes, sir."

"Cross-examine," Burger said.

"To the best of your knowledge, you had never seen the defendant before that time?" Mason asked.

"That's right, I had never seen her."

"You remember describing what had taken place to me in an oral report which you made?"

"Yes, sir."

"That was when the facts were more fresh in your mind?"

"They were fresh in my mind then, and they're fresh in my mind now."

161

"But they were *more* fresh at that time?"

"Perhaps. I suppose they must have been. Not that I can see it makes any difference."

"But they were?"

"Well . . . yes, they were."

"All right. Now at that time when you described the person who walked down the corridor to me, didn't you say that the thing you mainly noticed about her was her legs?"

"No, sir. I don't think I did."

"Didn't you say in describing her that she appeared to be two-thirds stockings?"

"Well, I guess I did."

"And do you want this jury to understand that under those circumstances you *weren't* looking at her legs?"

Faulkner shifted his position, grinned, and said, "I looked her all over."

"When did you next see this defendant?"

"On the eighteenth when she walked into the shadow box."

"Who was present at that time?"

"Sergeant Dorset, another detective, and Sam Meeker, the house detective of the Richmell Hotel."

"Anyone else?"

"No, sir, that's all. There was a police officer who kept records, sitting over by the entrance to the shadow box."

"Just describe that shadow box, if you will, please."

"Well, it's a brilliantly lighted stage, with lines ruled along the back of it, lines that enable you to tell a person's height. There's a line for five feet, and then there are lines for every inch about five feet up until six feet seven."

"And you say this is brilliantly lighted?"

"That's right."

"What else?"

"There's a curtain of white material, something like cheesecloth only it isn't cheesecloth, that hangs down in front and that's lighted. Then the room in which the officers sit is dark so that the person who is being identified can't tell who is out there on the other side of the curtain. The persons to

162

be identified are brought into the box and made to walk around a little bit and talk.''

"What about?"

"It doesn't make any difference. Just talk so that the people who are watching can hear the sound of the voice and detect the mannerisms of speaking.''

"And you saw the defendant in that box?"

"Yes, sir."

"On the eighteenth?"

"That's right."

"And identified her?"

"Absolutely."

"And you say Samuel Meeker was there?"

"Yes, sir."

"He identified her?"

"He did, both of us together identified her."

"Without any hesitancy?"

"Without any hesitancy."

"You noticed the way she was dressed?"

"Yes, sir."

"You knew that those were the same clothes the person whom you had seen in the hotel corridor early in the morning of the seventeenth was wearing?"

"That's right. Yes, sir."

"The same legs?" Mason asked.

The witness grinned. "The same legs."

"You heard her voice?"

"Well, now, wait a minute," the witness said. "I heard her voice, but I don't think that I heard it clearly the first time I saw her in the shadow box."

"There was more than one occasion?"

"Yes, sir."

"What was the occasion of having her return to the shadow box?"

"There was some question in Sergeant Dorset's mind, I believe, about the way she acted. There was an argument . . ."

"I object," Hamilton Burger said. "I've let this examination ramble far afield, your Honour, in the interest of saving time, but this witness certainly cannot testify as to what was in the mind of Sergeant Dorset. That is something Sergeant Dorset can testify to, if it is pertinent. The witness cannot testify to it."

"That's right," Judge Donahue said. "The objection is sustained. It is, at best, a conclusion of the witness."

"Sergeant Dorset himself told me . . ."

"That makes no difference," Judge Donahue said. "That's only hearsay."

"Well," Mason asked, "did *you* yourself notice anything?"

"I noticed that the first time she entered the shadow box she hadn't talked clearly. She'd been rather sullen and noncooperative and kept her head down and Sergeant Dorset didn't like the appearance she'd made. He said that the officer who was on duty at the time . . . well, I guess I'm not allowed to testify to the things they said."

"There was an argument?" Mason asked.

"I'll say there was, and finally the man in charge said to Sergeant Dorset, 'Well, if you think you can do it any better, suppose you try it,' or something like that, and Dorset said by gosh he would, and then he had the girl brought back."

"You had been waiting in the shadow room all the time?"

"No, no, we'd been out talking in the police station and then before we went home Dorset said he didn't like the way the girl had been put in the shadow box and asked us to excuse him a while, and we sat there and waited for about fifteen or twenty minutes, or maybe a little longer, and then Dorset came back and said the more he thought of it the less satisfied he became. Then he sent for the officer who had been in charge of the shadow box and they had quite an argument."

"All this, of course," Hamilton Burger said, "is purely hearsay as to what Sergeant Dorset said. I objected to it before, but it seems it will take less time to let the witness get it out of his system."

"Do you wish to move to strike it out?"

"I don't," Burger said, "although it has no place cluttering up the record. I just want the jury to realize it's hearsay and utterly irrelevant."

"Move to strike it out and it'll go out," Judge Donahue said.

"Oh, leave it in," Burger said magnanimously, waving his hand as though he were perfectly willing to surrender all technicalities in the interests of getting speedy justice and a fair verdict.

Mason, interested, asked the witness, "Was there some bitterness between these police officers?"

"There certainly was."

"Good Lord," Hamilton Burger said, "this is so far afield it isn't even connected by the most remote link of hearsay speculation."

"It certainly is not proper cross-examination," Judge Donahue rebuked. "Counsel is entitled to show the circumstances under which the identification took place, but irrelevant communications between police officers concerning the manner in which police procedure is carried out certainly can have no bearing on this case. However, gentlemen, I see that it has now reached the hour of five o'clock, which is the hour of the evening adjournment, and I'm going to remand the defendant. The jury will be in the custody of the sheriff. I take it arrangements have been made for hotel accommodations, Sheriff?"

"Yes, your Honour."

"Very well," the Judge said, "I will swear you to faithfully keep the jury in your custody and charge."

Judge Donahue swore the sheriff, then turned to the jurors and said, "You jurors are particularly cautioned not to form or express any opinion as to the merits of the controversy or the guilt or innocence of the defendant until all the evidence is before you. You are warned not to discuss this case among yourselves, or permit it to be discussed in your presence. You will not separate, nor permit yourselves to be addressed. You will be in the custody of the sheriff. Every attempt will be made to make you comfortable, but until this case is finished you will of necessity be in the custody of the sheriff. Inasmuch as any violation of my instructions would be reason for a mistrial which would be expensive to the state and might well jeopardize the rights of the parties, I am asking you to cooperate with me in order to see that nothing of this sort occurs. Court is adjourned until ten o'clock tomorrow morning.''

Mason, leaving his seat at the defendant's counsel table, walked rapidly up to the clerk's desk. "Let me take a look at that fan, will you, please?''

He carefully examined the fan which had been introduced in evidence, then turned back to where Lois Fenton was standing by the side of the deputy.

"Just a moment," Mason said to the deputy. "I want to talk with my client for a moment, please.''

He took Lois Fenton's arm, escorted her over a few feet out of earshot, said in a low voice, "I notice that fan was made by a firm in St. Louis. Are all fans used by fan-dancers made there?''

"No, I don't think so. Why?''

"Because," Mason said, "I found two fans in an automobile. I advertised them and Cherie Chi-Chi claimed them. She described them perfectly and I turned them over to her. She . . .''

Lois Fenton became excited. "Was this fan one of them?''

"I'm quite certain it was.''

"It's one of my fans. I'm very much attached to it. I have my initials stamped in gold on the bottom part.''

"I noticed," Mason said. "I feel quite certain this is one of the fans I turned over to Cherie Chi-Chi only a few hours before the murder. How did you happen to lose it?''

"I didn't lose it. They were at the ranch. John had taken them for safekeeping. When I left, I tried to get the fans, and he wouldn't give them to me, so I had to buy other fans. They weren't what I wanted—and I've always had a feeling that these fans brought me luck. That's why John gave them to Irene.''

Mason said, "The thing becomes important, Lois. If we can prove that this is one of the fans that was turned over to Irene and that you didn't see it again until . . .''

Mason's voice trailed off into silence.

"Yes?'' she asked.

Mason shook his head. "That story about how you came by the fan is too damn fantastic. It just doesn't ring true."

"But it's the truth, Mr. Mason."

Mason said, "Well, truth or not, one thing's certain. It's exceedingly important to show that this fan was not in your possession at the time the murder was committed. You hadn't seen it from the time you left your husband until . . . Damn it, I wish there were some logical way of accounting for the manner in which that fan came into your possession . . . and trying to bury it. That evidence hangs you. What about this shadow box business?" Mason asked. "Were you put in the shadow box twice?"

"That's right. They put me in the box twice."

"And the second time was within half an hour of the first time?"

"I would say just about half an hour. But they're wrong about saying that I was sulky. I wasn't."

Mason said, "Well, the important thing is to find out why they put you back in the shadow box the second time. What the police argument was about. Of course, you couldn't see anything on the other side of that curtain?"

"No. The lights are on that curtain so that it completely dazzles your eyes. You can't see anything at all in the room outside. You get a faint suggestion of motion in the darkness; that is, you know that people are out there, but you can't see them. You can't tell how many people or who they are, or anything about them."

"When did they put you in the shadow box, Lois?"

"The first time was almost immediately after I'd been arrested. They picked me up in—well you know, in your car."

Mason nodded.

"And they rushed me up to the jail and then before they booked me or anything they rushed me into this shadow box. Then they took me out and fingerprinted me and all that stuff. I guess that's what they call 'booking a prisoner.' "

Again Mason nodded.

"And then they took me back to the shadow box the second time."

"It may have been someone's idea that they didn't have

167

any right to put you in the shadow box before you were booked,'' Mason said. "I can't figure it. However, it was just one of those things that happen. I'd just like to know why it was done.''

"You don't think it's the reason that Sergeant Dorset gave?''

"I don't know,'' Mason said. "The thing I do know is that burying that fan absolutely crucifies you. You've got to account for that or you're a gone goose.''

"I guess I'm a gone goose, then,'' she said, attempting to smile. "I told you all about the fan. Arthur gave it to me.''

"You can't make a jury believe that story, Lois.''

"Why not?''

"Because you can't even make *me* believe it, and I'm your lawyer.''

Without a word she turned away and said to the deputy, "I'm ready.''

Chapter 19

Mason, pacing the floor of his office with Paul Drake and Della Street watching him in silence, threw words out in jerky sentences, interspersed with periods of silence.

"We've got to find this other fan-dancer. There's something screwy about that whole business . . . The fan is one of those that I gave to Cherie Chi-Chi."

Drake said, "Don't butt your head against a brick wall, Perry. The fan does it. She's hooked."

"I know she's hooked, the way things are right now."

There was an interval of silence during which Mason slowly and thoughtfully paced back and forth. Then, at length he said, "Hang it, Paul, we've simply *got* to find Cherie Chi-Chi."

"We're doing everything we can. She seems to have vanished absolutely," Drake said. "I've had men working until they're ready to drop, but we can't seem to get a single line. The woman's simply disappeared."

"When?"

"About twenty-four hours after Sergeant Holcomb picked her up and took her in for questioning. She came back to her apartment late on the afternoon of the eighteenth. I had a man covering the place. She was in there about half an hour, then came out with a suitcase. A cab picked her up. My man started to follow the cab, and then ran into an unlucky break. A traffic cop picked him up for turning out into a line of traffic without waiting for a break in the line. By the time he'd explained, the cab was gone. My man wasted time trying to find her. I didn't get his report until late."

Mason frowned. "Are you sure it was just an unlucky break, Paul?"

"You mean the cop might have been waiting so he could give this fan-dancer a getaway?"

Mason nodded.

"It's a thought," Drake admitted after a moment. "I don't see how it could really have been like that, but it's something to think over."

"What happened at Barlow's office, Paul? Did you get a line on that?"

Drake said, "Your trap worked like a charm, Perry. As soon as you left Barlow's office, they destroyed Lois Fenton's pictures and prepared to swear there never had been but one fan-dancer on their bookings and that was Irene. When Dorset swooped down they thought he was investigating the fraud angle. They told him Cherie Chi-Chi and Lois Fenton were one and the same person, showed him pictures and called in Cherie Chi-Chi.

"Dorset took her along for questioning. However, he evidently believed her story. He didn't book her but went after Lois. Irene simply vanished."

Mason, who had paused momentarily, resumed his pacing of the floor. "We simply *have* to find that woman."

"What would you do with her if you got her?" Drake asked. "She's hostile."

"It wouldn't make any difference," Mason said. "I'd put her on the stand and ask her a few questions."

"By the time you find her and get her on the stand," Drake said grimly, "she won't look any more like Lois Fenton than Della Street does. She'll be wearing a demure long skirt and butter won't melt in her mouth."

"That'll suit me fine, Paul. I'll ask her where the clothes are that she was wearing on the date of the murder. I'll ask her to describe them. And then I'll ask her if they didn't resemble the clothes the defendant is wearing. I'll crucify her with that stuff, and then demand that she be attired in the clothes she wore on the day of the murder."

"Yes, I guess you can make quite a diversion there," Drake said, "but that's all it'll be. These witnesses have all identified Lois, and they sure as hell aren't going to switch now."

Knuckles tapped on the door to Mason's private office, at first tentatively, then, when there was no answer, more imperatively.

Mason glanced at Della Street, nodded.

Della opened the door. A man's voice said, "Hello, Miss Street."

"Why . . . Mr. Faulkner!"

Drake came up out of his chair in a single quick motion. "Hello, Frank. What the hell?"

Faulkner said, "Excuse me for interrupting, but I wanted to talk with you."

"Come on in," Mason invited cordially.

Faulkner entered the room. The door slowly closed behind him and clicked shut.

Faulkner grinned somewhat sheepishly at Mason. "I suppose you think I've sold you out?"

"I appreciate your position, Faulkner."

"He understands," Paul Drake said, hastily. "No one ran to the police and blabbed. The police ran to us."

Faulkner said, "I thought possibly I could make up for it in a way."

"How?" Mason asked.

Faulkner walked over to one of the chairs, calmly sat down and crossed his legs. "Now you understand," he said, "there's nothing unethical about this, but I'd just as soon no one knew where the information came from. The police have a legal right to tell a detective to kick through with information when a murder is involved and the detective is a witness, but on the other hand the police don't have any right to insist that a detective *suppress* information."

Mason nodded.

"Well," Faulkner went on, "I just thought that you'd want to know where this Cherie Chi-Chi is. The police have her."

"What!" Mason asked, incredulously.

"That's right, the police have her."

"On what charge?"

"I'm damned if I know, but I think it's some sort of a deal."

"You mean she's remaining in confinement willingly?"

"That's my idea."

"How do you know?"

"What the hell," Faulkner said, "I've seen her, talked with her."

"When?"

"Two or three times."

"Who else has seen her and talked with her, do you know?"

"Sam Meeker."

"What's the idea?" Drake asked.

"The idea's plain enough," Mason said, bitterly, "and it's so damn simple I should have thought of it. That's one of Sergeant Holcomb's smart tricks. I doubt if Lieutenant Tragg would pull a stunt like that."

"Holcomb's the one who's engineering the thing," Faulkner said.

"I still don't get it," Drake said.

"Simple enough," Mason said. "They figure that somewhere along the line I may be able to get Cherie Chi-Chi into court. I might make some dramatic presentation that would confuse the witnesses. But if the witnesses have previously been given an opportunity to become well acquainted with her, they won't make any mistake. Not only are they acquainted now with Lois Fenton, but they've had an opportunity to see Cherie Chi-Chi. The two girls are alike as two peas as far as figure and build and complexion are concerned, but their features aren't the same and there's no particular resemblance there."

Faulkner said, "Well, I thought I'd let you know. It seemed to me that you had a break coming and I decided I could spill this information. The police don't have any right to tell a man to keep something to himself."

"How was Cherie Chi-Chi dressed when you saw her? Anything like Lois Fenton?"

"Not the first two times," Faulkner said. "The last time she was."

"Can you tell us any more about that?" Mason asked.

"Well," Faulkner said, "it's like this. After we'd seen this girl and talked with her a couple of time, Sergeant Holcomb came to us and asked us if we thought we'd be confused in the event we saw this person wearing the same clothes that Lois Fenton was wearing, or clothes which were exactly the same.''

"What did you tell him?''

"We both told him we didn't think there was a chance in the world.''

"Sergeant Holcomb pointed out that the girl had the same build and the same general appearance; that if she were wearing the same clothes it might be that a witness would make a mistake.''

"So then what happened?''

"He took us up to a room in the detention ward and this Cheri Chi-Chi walked around for us. He told her to walk like Lois Fenton and damned if she didn't, but, of course, it wasn't Lois.''

"Now look here,'' Mason said, "is there any chance that this Cheri Chi-Chi could have been the one you saw in the corridor?''

Faulkner lit a cigarette. He said, "I've been thinking that over.''

"Let's think it over some more,'' Mason said.

"At first I'd have said one hundred percent 'no,' '' Faulkner told him. "Their faces are a lot different, but their figures are about the same and they've got the same general colouring. To tell you the truth, Mason, I . . . well, I would say that the girl I saw in the corridor was Lois Fenton, but . . .''

"I know,'' Mason said, "the way the build-up has been made, you'd naturally think that. You've had an opportunity to get familiar with Cherie Chi-Chi's appearance when she wasn't dressed at all like Lois Fenton, so that when you saw her dressed as Lois Fenton you weren't even confused.''

"That's the way Sam Meeker feels,'' Faulkner admitted, "but I keep thinking the thing over. If that Cherie Chi-Chi were brought into court—well, hang it, I *could* have made a mistake. I don't think I *did*, but I *could* have.''

"When did you see her dressed in these clothes?''

"About half an hour after the court adjourned. Sergeant Holcomb said that he thought the defence was laying a trap for us; that you were considered pretty foxy when it came to taking a witness by surprise. Not so much by questions as by some dramatic means that would tend to confuse us.''

"So you went up and saw Cherie Chi-Chi wearing these clothes that were identical with those worn by Lois Fenton?''

"That's right.''

"What did you say?''

"Well, at the time I told Holcomb I didn't think there was any chance I could have made a mistake, and Meeker said he knew damn well *he* couldn't have made a mistake, but—well, you get to thinking things over.''

"Anyone see you come here?'' Mason asked.

"You're damned right they didn't,'' Faulkner said. "I thought they might be having me tailed and I took care to see I wasn't spotted.''

"Okay,'' Mason said. "You'd better get out while the coast is still clear. I want to think this over.''

"I'm on my way,'' Faulkner said. ". . . you'll protect me in this thing, Mason?''

"Sure thing.''

Faulkner shook hands.

When he had gone, Mason turned to Drake. "Well, that's a break! I'll make a demand on the prosecution to produce Cherie Chi-Chi.''

"When?'' Drake asked.

Mason said, "Court will convene at ten o'clock tomorrow morning and promptly at 10.01 A.M. you are going to see the damnedest set of legal fireworks you ever witnessed.''

Chapter 20

The bailiff announced that Court had been called to order. Judge Donahue intoned the usual formula. "Gentlemen, it is stipulated that the jury are all present and the defendant in court?"

"So stipulated," Mason said.

"So stipulated," Burger announced.

Mason arose. "Your Honour, before we proceed with the trial of this case, I have a matter which I wish to call to the attention of the Court. It concerns a witness, a potential witness for the defence. We have been unable to find this witness no matter how we searched, and . . ."

"Give me the name of the witness," Burger said. "Tell me what you expect to prove by him and perhaps I will stipulate to it."

Mason said, "The name of the witness is Irene Kilby. She has, however, gone under the professional name of Cherie Chi-Chi and more lately has for some time been masquerading under the name of Lois Fenton. She has used clothes that are identical in appearance to those of Lois Fenton, she has made appearances under the name of Lois Fenton and has in every way tried to arrange her appearance so that she can be mistaken for Lois Fenton. We propose to prove that she, this witness, was in the Richmell Hotel on the night of the murder at the hour of approximately 2.20 in the morning."

"And how do you propose to prove that?"

"By the witness herself."

"It will be interesting to see you try," Burger said.

Judge Donahue frowned. "I fail to see the necessity of making such a statement at this time and in front of this jury, Mr. Mason."

"The reason I am making this statement, your Honour, is that I have just discovered that the reason we have been unable to find this witness no matter how much we searched, is that the police have been holding her incommunicado."

"Do you mean that the police have been concealing her?" Burger demanded indignantly.

"As far as we're concerned, yes."

"Your Honour, I resent that. The law specifically gives the prosecution the power to hold material witnesses and this is a material witness for the prosecution."

"I challenge that statement," Mason said.

Burger, red in the face, shouted, "I'll make it again. This woman is a material witness."

"You admit that she was kept concealed under such circumstances that I would not be able to find out where she was?" Mason asked.

"We don't have to write you every day and tell you what we intend to do in putting on our case," Burger said. "I say, your Honour, that this woman is a material witness."

"What's she a witness to?" Mason asked.

"To certain things that she will disclose when she gets on the stand."

"You don't intend to put her on the stand."

"I do."

"Put her on now then," Mason said.

Burger said, "I don't have to put her on now."

"Go ahead," Mason challenged. "If she's a witness to anything for you, put her on that witness stand. Let's hear what she has to say. Then you'll be finished with her and I can talk to her and put her on the stand as a witness for the defence."

Judge Donahue looked questioningly at Hamilton Burger.

"I'll put her on the witness stand when I get good and ready," Hamilton Burger said.

"Will you promise this court that you *are going* to put her on the witness stand?"

"I don't have to make any such promises."

"There you are, your Honour. The woman is not a witness."

Judge Donahue said, "After all, Mr. District Attorney, while the order of the proof ordinarily is in the hands of the district attorney, it certainly seems to me that if this woman is a material witness for the prosecution, and the defence desires to question her, that it would be much better to have the prosecution put her on the stand, take her testimony, and then release her so that the defence would be in a position to use her in the event they wished to do so."

"The defence doesn't want to use her, your Honour. This is simply a grandstand."

"I want to use her," Mason insisted.

"What do you propose to prove by her? Perhaps I'll stipulate it."

Mason said, "I propose to prove by the witness that she was the one whom the witnesses have identified as being the defendant, the woman who was in this hotel at twenty minutes past two o'clock in the morning."

"You can't do it," Burger said, "because these witnesses would know in a minute that this woman wasn't the defendant."

Mason said, "Bring her into court. Bring her in, dressed just as she was dressed when the woman was arrested, and by that I mean wearing clothes that were identical in cut, colour, pattern and texture to those worn by the defendant."

"All right," Burger snapped. "You've asked for this. I'll bring her into court. I'll give you every opportunity. Your Honour, if we may have fifteen minutes I think at that time I will be able to grant counsel's request. I will have Irene Kilby in court. I'll let her parade up in front of the witnesses. Perhaps in the meantime, I can save time by calling another witness, Jasper Fenton. Come forward and be sworn Jasper."

Jasper Fenton, a droop-shouldered lad, who had an expression of bored cynicism deeply stamped upon his countenance, took the witness stand. He answered the preliminary questions in a monotone. Then as Burger began to bring him to the scene of the crime, the boy's voice took on a slight nervousness.

"Where were you on the morning of the seventeenth of

September this year?'' Burger asked. ''Were you in the Rich-mell Hotel?''

''Yes, sir.''

''At what time?''

''I believe it was exactly 2.44.''

''Where did you go?''

''I went to John Callender's room. I mean I entered that room at approximately 2.44.''

''When did you leave?''

''Immediately.''

''*Why* did you leave?''

''I opened the door and saw him lying there, dead on the floor. I got out of there fast.''

''You had an appointment with him?''

''Yes, sir.''

''When did you have that appointment?''

''It wasn't exactly an appointment. He sent for me to come and see him.''

''What time were you supposed to be there?''

''At two o'clock in the morning.''

''That was a definite appointment?''

''Yes. He said I was to be there at two on the second.''

''But you were late?''

''Yes, sir.''

''Why were you late?''

''I stopped for a few drinks to bolster my courage. I didn't want to face him.''

''Why?''

''He was trying to blackmail my sister through me.''

''And by your sister you mean Lois Fenton, the defendant here?''

''Yes, sir.''

''She is your sister?''

''Yes, sir.''

''Let's be frank about this,'' Hamilton Burger said. ''John Callender had some hold on you?''

''Yes, he did.''

''What was it?''

Fenton squirmed about on the witness chair. ''I had been

178

working for him. I had forged his name to some cheques in order to cover a shortage. He had those cheques. He was threatening to prosecute me."

"Anything else?"

"When he kept hounding my sister through me, I became desperate. I took my sister's horse and went to John Callender's ranch. I rode up to the house and managed to get into the room where his records were kept. I had the safe opened when a night watchman came along the porch and saw my flashlight. He put the beam of his own flashlight through the window, spotted me at the safe and shouted for help. I ran out of the house, along the veranda, jumped into the saddle and started away at a gallop. The watchman shot."

"What happened to the bullet?"

"It grazed the horse and lodged in the saddle."

"You felt the impact of that bullet? You felt it hit?"

"Yes, sir. I felt the jar of the impact in the saddle. I knew the bullet was in the saddle."

"Did you subsequently make an investigation to find that it was embedded in the saddle?"

"Yes, sir."

"And what did you do?"

"I became panic-stricken. I got off the horse and hit it with the quirt until it ran away. Then I hitchhiked back home."

"Now you're not trying to conceal anything," Hamilton Burger said unctuously. "You're not trying to minimize your own shortcomings. Disagreeable as it is, you're admitting on the witness stand that you have committed forgery, that you went to John Callender's house and tried to burglarize the safe?"

"Yes, sir."

"And Callender knew about that?"

"Yes, sir."

"And what was he trying to do?"

"He was trying to force my sister to return by threatening to bring action against me."

"And he wanted to discuss that with you?"

"He didn't want to discuss anything with me, he wanted to *tell* me."

"And when you found John Callender lying there in that room dead, a Japanese sword plunged through his chest, you simply thought about escaping and got out of there without notifying anyone about what you had discovered. Is that right?"

"Yes, sir. That's only partially right."

"What's wrong with it?"

"After I got to thinking it over. After . . . well, the next day . . . I went to the police."

"Of your own accord? Is that right?"

"Yes, sir."

"And gave the police a written statement?"

"Yes, sir."

"And at that time," Burger went on suavely, "you didn't know that your sister was involved in any way? You didn't know she was accused of the crime, did you?"

"Just a moment," Mason said. "That question is viciously leading and suggestive. It is incompetent, irrelevant and immaterial. It's a self-serving declaration."

"It goes to the motivation and interest of the witness, if the Court please," Burger said.

"And as such, it's a question that can only be asked on cross-examination, and by opposing counsel," Mason said.

Judge Donahue said, "The question is leading, but I think I'll overrule the objection. I think the jury are entitled to the facts of the case."

"No, at that time I didn't know my sister was involved," the witness said.

"And you gave the police a written statement?"

"Yes, sir."

"So that you're really an unwilling witness and are giving your testimony with reluctance?"

Mason said, "He isn't giving his testimony, if the Court please. The District Attorney is giving it for him. Your Honour, I protest that the District Attorney keeps feeding this stuff into the record and all the witness is supposed to do is to say 'yes.' "

"These questions *are* viciously leading," Judge Donahue said. "The record will show, I'm afraid, that the District Attorney has been guilty of leading the witnesses many times. The objection is sustained. We will have no further leading questions."

"Cross-examine," Burger snapped.

Mason started to get to his feet when there was a commotion in the courtroom. A deputy sheriff caught Burger's eye and gave a signal. Burger said, "If the Court please, the witness, Irene Kilby, is now in court, brought here at the suggestion, in fact at the demand, of Perry Mason. Now then, if Mr. Mason wishes to talk with this witness, he is at perfect liberty to do so. If, as I suspect to be the case, he only wishes to use her as a means of confusing the witnesses who have already testified, I have no objection to any test he may desire to make. Come forward, Miss Kilby, so the jury and the witnesses may see you."

Irene Kilby came forward, walking now not like Lois Fenton, but holding her hips stiff, her head and chin up.

Judge Donahue regarded her at first with mild interest, then, suddenly puzzled, looked from her to Lois Fenton. He said, "Will the defendant please stand up. Now stand over there, the two of you together. Any objection, Mr. Mason?"

"None, your Honour."

Judge Donahue looked at the two women. "Well, this is indeed a strange situation. There is no great facial resemblance, but as far as figures are concerned, it is a different situation. These two women are apparently exactly identical as to height and shape and are wearing identical apparel. Do you care to make a statement, Mr. Burger?"

Hamilton Burger said, "Your Honour, I should have known that Perry Mason would make some spectacular grandstand . . ."

"Never mind that," Judge Donahue interrupted. "I simply want to know what is the occasion for this very evident masquerade on the part of these young women. The defendant may be seated. I am going to ask the witness Irene Kilby to remain here for the moment. Just remain standing, if you will, Miss Kilby. Now, Mr. Burger."

Hamilton Burger said, "Your Honour, I now offer to stipulate facts that Mr. Mason knows to be true, that this witness used the name of Lois Fenton, and dressed herself so that she looked like Lois Fenton for reasons that, however, are quite obvious once the situation is understood."

"Well, I should like to know what they are."

Burger said, "This young woman wanted to be a fandancer. Lois Fenton was a very successful fan-dancer. Lois Fenton married and thereby terminated her career as a fandancer. At the time of her marriage she had several unfulfilled contracts . . . May I go on?"

"I am willing to listen to anything the District Attorney may have to say," Judge Donahue said, "subject, of course, to the fact that the defendant has the right to object to this procedure. Is there any objection, Mr. Mason?"

Mason said, "I have no objection to Hamilton Burger giving testimony, if he is under oath. Then I want to cross-examine him just as I would any witness. I have no objection to his making a preliminary explanation to your Honour, but as far as the question of fact is concerned as to what actuated this witness to do the things she did do, the witness herself is the one to give the evidence."

"But it's no part of the case," Hamilton Burger said, his voice and manner showing his exasperation. "I'm simply explaining the preliminaries to his Honour at the Court's own request."

"If it isn't part of the case," Mason asked, "why did you detain this woman as a material witness? What's she a witness to?"

"I detained her so that you couldn't . . ."

"Yes, yes, go on," Mason said temptingly, as Burger stopped suddenly. "You were about to blurt out the *real* reason for her detention."

"That will do, gentlemen," Judge Donahue said. "The occasion requires no interchange between counsel. The Court is merely asking for information and if counsel for the defence objects to any statement being made by the District Attorney in this manner, it will be necessary, of course, to put this young woman on the stand."

"But this is attempting to prove a negative," Hamilton Burger said. "It is only important in the event the defence claims that this masquerade fooled somebody; that is, that it had the effect of confusing the witnesses."

"I claim it did," Mason said.

"Go ahead and prove that it did then," Burger challenged.

Judge Donahue said, "One thing at a time, gentlemen. Now, do I understand, Mr. Mason, that you object to this statement by Hamilton Burger?"

"Provided that it is only preliminary, I have no objection to it, but if Hamilton Burger seeks by such a statement to obviate the necessity of putting this woman on the stand, I do object to it. I will further say that I stipulate to nothing. This witness is going on the stand as far as I'm concerned."

"Well," Judge Donahue said, "perhaps we'd better proceed in the regular way, but this certainly is a peculiar situation which has developed, and the Court felt that it might be better to have it explained."

Mason said, "In view of the fact that this young woman is here, I now ask the privilege of recalling Samuel Meeker for cross-examination."

"I have no objection in the world," Burger said, with a sarcastic bow at Perry Mason. "Go right ahead."

"That will do, Mr. Burger," Judge Donahue said. "Can't we try this case without interchange of comments between counsel? Now, where were we? Oh yes, we want Sam Meeker on the stand. Mr. Samuel Meeker, come back to the stand. No, no, you've already been sworn. Just sit down there in that chair. You want to cross-examine him further, Mr. Mason?"

"I do. Miss Kilby, I would like to have you walk back and forth across the courtroom directly in front of the counsel table here, where the witness can see you."

Irene Kilby dutifully walked back and forth.

"Not that way," Mason said. "The way you customarily walk."

She looked at him with wide eyes. "I'm afraid I don't know how that is, Mr. Mason."

"With a swing of the hips, a certain voluptuous entice-ment. Certainly you always walked that way before . . ."

"Your Honour, I object to that," Hamilton Burger said. "Counsel has asked the witness to walk. She has walked. If Perry Mason wants to swear that he has seen this witness walk with a swaying of the hips or in a voluptuous manner, he himself can take the oath and get on the witness stand, and then *I* will cross-examine *him*."

"Counsel has asked the witness to walk in a certain par-ticular manner," Judge Donahue said, "but I am not satis-fied that counsel has the right to do that in connection with a test of this nature. He has asked Miss Kilby to walk, and she has walked. I think that is as far as the Court should permit an experiment of this kind to be carried out until there is some evidence showing the young woman may at some other time have walked in some other manner."

"Very well," Mason said. "Now, Mr. Meeker, is there any possibility that this young woman whom you see now before you, referring to Irene Kilby, is the woman who came to the Richmell Hotel at approximately 2.20 in the morning and . . ."

"None whatever."

"Let me finish my question. And was stopped by you at the elevators, or near the elevators, and taken by you over to the telephones where a call was put through to the room of John Callender?"

"There is no possibility whatever."

"You're positive?"

"Positive."

"You recognize a certain resemblance to the defendant?"

"There's a resemblance as far as clothes are concerned, and a resemblance as far as figures are concerned, but this is Irene Kilby, and I'd recognize her anywhere. The defen-dant is the woman whom I saw in the hotel, and I'd recognize *her* anywhere."

"When did you last see Irene Kilby?" Mason asked.

"Yesterday afternoon."

"And before that?"

"I don't know. Yesterday morning, I guess."

"And you have seen her on several occasions immediately before the trial of this action?"

"Yes."

"What was the reason for so seeing her?"

"Well, Sergeant Dorset wanted to be certain that she *wasn't* the woman I'd seen. He kept showing her to me and asking me if there was any possibility of my being mistaken."

"Oh I see," Mason said. "In other words, the police used every means to see that you would be fully familiar with the features of this Irene Kilby so that in the event you were suddenly confronted with her in court you wouldn't be confused. Is that it?"

"Objected to," Burger snapped. "Calling for a conclusion—argumentative."

"Sustained."

"And before Sergeant Dorset took you to Irene Kilby he took some pains to impress upon you that this was Irene Kilby and not the Lois Fenton whom you had already identified, is that right?" Mason asked.

"Well, he told me."

"That's all," Mason said.

"No questions," Burger said.

"Proceed with the case," Judge Donahue said to Burger.

"Jasper Fenton was on the stand. Mr. Mason was about to start his cross-examination," Burger said.

"If the Court please," Mason interposed, "as I understand it the District Attorney is going to put this young woman on the witness stand."

Burger said, "You've already covered everything that I wanted to have covered."

"But you were holding her as a *material* witness," Mason said.

"Well, what of it?"

"In the event you were keeping her out of circulation where I couldn't find her, and where my men couldn't interview her, you were abusing the judicial processes of this Court."

"You've said that before," Burger said.

"And I'm going to say it again," Mason said. "I just don't

want to have any misunderstanding on that point. You either call that witness to the stand, or you can explain to the grievance committee why you were holding her where I couldn't find her, claiming she was a material witness.''

Burger thought that over, then suddenly surrendered. 'Irene Kilby take the stand,'' he said angrily, his face red.

"Your true name is Irene Kilby?'' Burger asked, when the witness had been sworn.

"Yes, sir.''

"Have you ever gone under any other name?''

"Yes, sir.''

"What?''

"Two names. The name of Cherie Chi-Chi, which is a stage name, and the name of Lois Fenton.''

"How did it happen that you went under the name of Lois Fenton?''

"She told me I might.''

"You mean the young woman sitting there at the right of Mr. Mason, the woman who is the defendant in the case of The People *vs.* Lois Fenton, told you that you could use her name?''

"Yes, sir.''

"And what did she tell you? Describe that conversation.''

"She told me . . .''

"Just a moment,'' Mason interrupted. "Was there a written agreement?''

"Yes, sir.''

"Then the agreement, the writing itself, is the best evidence,'' Mason said.

Burger frowned. "Where is that writing, Miss Kilby?''

"I don't know.''

"Why don't you know?''

"I surrendered it to John Callender and I have never seen it since.''

"When did you surrender it?''

"A few days before his death.''

"And you have searched for it and been unable to find it?''

"Yes.''

186

"Very well, then, tell us what was in it."

"Well, I was trying to get on as a fan-dancer, and I didn't have many engagements. Lois Fenton had a full calendar. She didn't want to go ahead with her fan-dancing when she got married, so I asked her if I couldn't fill her dates, and she told me I could. I told her I'd have to use her name, and she said that would be all right."

"Very well. Now, at any time on the morning of September seventeenth did you go to the Richmell Hotel?"

"Yes, sir. I went there shortly before two o'clock in the morning. That was the only time I ever went there."

"You saw John Callender then?"

"I did."

"And you talked with him?"

"Yes."

"What about?"

"I asked him for the agreement. He said he had given it to Lois. I left the room about two o'clock. A maid saw me as I left the room. I never went back."

"Did you seek Samuel Meeker, the house detective, at that hotel and have any conversation with him?"

"No, sir."

"Your witness," Burger snapped.

Mason arose to conduct the cross-examination.

"In order to carry out the deception incident upon your attempt to capitalize on Lois Fenton's good will as a fan-dancer, you copied her clothes, did you not?" he asked.

"Well, what's wrong with that?"

"But you did, didn't you?"

"Of course I did."

"Exactly why did you do that?"

"Because bookings were made through her agent, a Mr. Barlow, and Mr. Barlow had photographs."

"You mean Sidney Jackson Barlow?"

"Yes, sir."

"And you didn't want Mr. Barlow to think there had been any substitution or any change in his clients?"

"Naturally not."

"So you dressed just as much as you could like Lois Fenton and made yourself look just as much as you could like Lois Fenton, didn't you?''

''What would you have done under the same circumstances?''

''I'm asking *you* what *you* did. You did do that, didn't you?''

''Yes. It's obvious. I am wearing these clothes now.''

''And Mr. Barlow never raised the point that perhaps you were not the real Lois Fenton?''

''Not until after you had been there, trying to make trouble.''

''Now, then,'' Mason said, ''directing your attention to the evening of September seventeenth, you went to the office of Sidney Jackson Barlow, the agent, did you not?''

''I did.''

''And what happened to you there?''

''Incompetent, irrelevant and immaterial. Not proper cross-examination,'' Hamilton Burger said. ''Your Honour, this is wandering far afield. This is something that was not touched upon in direct examination and has nothing to do with the issues in this case.''

Judge Donahue glanced down at Perry Mason. ''It would seem to be highly incompetent, Counsellor.''

''If the Court please,'' Mason argued, ''I desire to show that at that time the officers arrested her as Lois Fenton; that she was at that time told she was arrested on suspicion of the murder of John Callender.''

''But what would that have to do with it?'' Judge Donahue asked. ''I am impressed with the most peculiar circumstances of this case. I am going to give you every latitude in your cross-examination in view of this evident masquerade, but I don't see exactly what competent matter could be brought out by such a question as you now ask. Assuming that a description of Lois Fenton had been broadcast and that this young woman undoubtedly answered that description, assuming further that the officers took her into custody under the mistaken impression that she was Lois Fenton, I still can't see any relevancy.''

''Simply this,'' Mason said. ''I propose to show that this

witness was thereupon taken to the jail, that the next day she was placed in a device known as a shadow box by which witnesses are enabled to view prisoners without the prisoners seeing them, and I propose to show, your Honour,'' Mason went on, his voice rising dramatically, *"that while she was in that shadow box she was identified absolutely by the witness Sam Meeker and the witness Frank Faulkner as the woman they had seen in the Richmell Hotel at the hour of approximately twenty minutes past two on the morning of September seventeenth!"*

"That's not so,'' Hamilton Burger shouted. "You can't prove it. You can't . . .''

"Give me a chance and I will,'' Mason said, grimly.

"But I don't understand,'' Judge Donahue said, frowning.

"I didn't for a moment, your Honour, but I understand now,'' Mason said. "The police arrested this woman as Lois Fenton. The next day the witnesses identified her as the woman they had seen in the hotel. Then, within a few minutes after that identification had been made, the police arrested the real Lois Fenton, so Sergeant Holcomb arranged for a second identification, telling the witnesses that they were going to see the girl again under more advantageous circumstances, and the witnesses both thought they were seeing the same girl. And in order to keep these witnesses from suspecting anything, these two police officers staged a fake quarrel so that when the witnesses entered that room containing the shadow box on that second occasion they were so fully convinced in advance that the woman they then saw was the same one they had already seen, they hardly gave her identity any real thought. And then, in order to keep me from finding out what had happened, the police later put the defendant, Lois Fenton, back in the shadow box for a second time. But at that time *there was no one on the other side of the screen.* That was a police trap, simply for the purpose of keeping me from finding out. . . .''

"That's not so!'' Hamilton Burger shouted.

"You'd better find out whether it's so or not before you start throwing denials around this courtroom,'' Mason said. "Interview the sergeant who had charge of the shadow box.

I don't think Lieutenant Tragg had any part in this, but you interview Sergeant Holcomb and see what he says. And incidentally, your Honour, noticing that Sergeant Holcomb is in court, I ask that he be required to remain as a witness for the defence until I can have an opportunity to have a subpoena issued and served upon him.''

Judge Donahue banged with his gavel, but all of his attempts to restore order were ineffectual. Sergeant Holcomb got to his feet, started to say something, turned, headed for the door, then paused.

Hamilton Burger shouted, "Holcomb, come here! I want to talk with you!"

Mason settled back in his chair and smiled reassuringly at the defendant.

"But how did you ever know?" Lois Fenton whispered.

Mason said, "What makes my face red is that I didn't know it long ago. The thing is obvious. They did put you in the shadow box on two occasions. But you didn't hang your head and sulk the first time. When the witnesses saw you for the first time, they thought they were seeing you for the second time.''

'Will that prove that Irene Kilby was the one who was in the hotel?''

"It will go a long way toward proving it," Mason said. "It'll prove that the first person the witnesses identified as being the one they saw in that hotel was Irene Kilby, and unless I am greatly mistaken that's going to raise merry hell.''

The Judge's gavel finally pounded the court to order.

Hamilton Burger said, "Your Honour, this is a most astounding statement that counsel has made. I cannot believe that it has any foundation in fact. Even if it has, it tends only to cast some slight doubt upon the identification, but it cannot defeat the . . .''

"The Court would like to know," Judge Donahue interrupted, "whether or not this witness Irene Kilby was put in the shadow box at a time when the witness Sam Meeker and the witness Frank Faulkner were there to make an identification.''

"Of course, your Honour, she can't tell. She doesn't know who was on the other side of the screen."

"Well, the police know!" Judge Donahue all but shouted, irritably.

"Yes, your Honour, and if I may have a recess I will endeavor to find out the true facts."

"How long a recess do you want?"

"An hour. Will that be convenient to the Court?"

"Make it until two o'clock this afternoon," Judge Donahue said. "We'll recess court until two o'clock this afternoon, and by that time I want to find out exactly what happened. After all, the police records are not available to the defendant in this case and this witness Irene Kilby certainly has been kept where she was inaccessible to the defence."

"As a material witness," Burger said. "And she was held at her own consent, your Honour."

Judge Donahue said, "I have no desire to criticize anyone until I have some basis for criticism, but I want to get at the bottom of this. Is there any objection to recess until two o'clock this afternoon, Mr. Mason?"

"There is, your Honour."

Judge Donahue frowned. "Obviously, Mr. Mason, the District Attorney must make certain investigations to find out what happened. He needs to consult certain records. The Court wishes to know what really happened on that shadow box identification. It would certainly seem that the defendant would be equally anxious to have the facts disclosed. Therefore, it seems to the Court the request for a recess is in order."

Mason said, "I agree with your Honour in principle, but the District Attorney has able assistants to handle routine matters. I am entitled to go on with my cross-examination of this witness before she is given time to confer with her friends and think up some new story to tell. A ten-minute recess will give the District Attorney ample opportunity to have his assistants get the police records and to confer with Sergeant Holcomb."

"Very well," Judge Donahue said, "if the defence wishes

191

to finish the cross-examination of these witnesses, it is entitled to do so. The Court will take a ten-minute recess.''

Paul Drake, pushing his way through the milling spectators, fought to Mason's side. ''Boy, oh boy, are you dishing it out!'' he exclaimed. ''But they've picked up Arthur Sheldon, Perry, so be careful. They may spring him as a witness.''

''Where is he?'' Mason asked.

''In the jail. They got him to waive extradition and brought him back. They handled it very secretly. The newspapers are being given the news now.''

Mason said, ''I wish he would take the stand. We're getting somewhere now.''

''And how!'' Drake said exultantly. ''Gosh, what a wallop, Perry! You've knocked them for a loop!''

Chapter 21

When Court reconvened a nervous, frightened Irene Kilby was on the witness stand and an exasperated District Attorney was quite evidently on the defensive. His manners plainly showed he was thoroughly angered at the police trick, which, by this time, Sergeant Holcomb had apparently confessed.

Mason said, "Now, Miss Kilby, you took the identity of Lois Fenton, you fulfilled her professional engagements, you dressed like her, is that right?"

"Yes, sir."

"You had an agreement with her and you surrendered that agreement to John Callender, is that right?"

"Yes, sir."

"And so far as you know, that was the only copy of that agreement in existence?"

"Yes, sir."

"You wanted to get possession of that agreement, didn't you?"

"I have already said so. Yes."

"And you made a search for it?"

"Yes."

"And isn't the real reason that you were so anxious to get that agreement because there was a clause in it providing that in the event Lois Fenton's marriage wasn't successful, or if at any time she wished to return to fan-dancing, you would step on one side?"

"No, sir."

"Or words to that effect were in that agreement?"

"No, sir."

"Think carefully, now," Mason said. "You're under oath. And remember, if John Callender had that agreement, sooner or later it is going to show up among the effects of his estate.

That is a written agreement. It is signed by Lois Fenton and it is signed by you. Now, just remember that you're under oath and that a lot more is involved here than your career as a fan-dancer.''

The witness bit her lip.

"Go on," Mason said. "Let's try making another answer to that question. Isn't that the *real* reason you wanted the agreement?''

The witness shifted her position, glanced helplessly at the District Attorney, then met the stern eyes of the judge.

"Well," Mason said, "isn't it?''

"Yes," she answered, in a low voice.

"Now," Mason said, "we're beginning to get somewhere. It was vital to your career to have that agreement, wasn't it?''

"Yes.''

"And as long as John Callender had it, he had you, in a very great measure, in his power, didn't he?''

"Yes.''

"Now, then," Mason went on, "let's go a little farther. This fan which I will show you, the one which has been introduced as People's Exhibit Number 2—take a good look at that fan. You will notice the initials 'L.F.' on it. You will notice that it was made in St. Louis. You have seen that fan before?''

"Yes.''

"I gave it to you, didn't I?''

"Yes.''

"When?''

"The night of the murder—that is, you gave it to me on the evening of the sixteenth, and John Callender was murdered shortly after midnight that same night, which makes it the seventeenth.''

"Exactly," Mason said. "Now, what did you do with that fan when I gave it to you? There were two of them, weren't there?''

"Yes.''

"And what did you do with them?''

"I . . . I gave them . . .''

"Yes, yes, go on," Mason said.

"I gave them to John Callender."

"Now did you give them to John Callender personally, or did you give them to Harry Cogswell to give to John Callender?"

"Harry was to give them to him."

"As soon as you got possession of those fans in Palomino, you and Harry Cogswell jumped into an automobile and drove just as fast as you could to report to John Callender that I hadn't found the horse he wanted, that I had found two fans, and in order to support your story you took those two fans to Cogswell, didn't you?"

"Yes."

"And you gave those fans to Cogswell to deliver to Callender?"

"Yes."

"And Cogswell arrived at the hotel about one-twenty and went to see Callender, and left the fans?"

"He left one of the fans. I had one."

Mason said, "For your information, Miss Kilby, and so I won't take any advantage of you, I will state that I personally saw Harry Cogswell entering Callender's room at approximately twenty minutes past one on the morning of the seventeenth. Now, is that about the time he went to the room, or do you know?"

"It was right about that time."

"Where were you?"

"I was outside in the car. He couldn't find a parking place near the hotel, so I drove around the block and Harry went in to talk with Callender. We probably could have found a parking place if we'd looked around, but we would have had to walk quite a ways, and—well, Callender wanted that fan just as quick as he could get it. He said he had to have it before two o'clock, and he wanted it just as soon as he could possibly get it."

"Then you had talked with Callender over the telephone?"

"Yes."

"As soon as I'd given you the fans?"

"Yes."

"Now," Mason said, "let's be frank about this thing, Miss Kilby. You've been trying to protect your own interests, but I think you've been unnecessarily cautious. Suppose I should tell you that I could prove that when you called on John Callender at 2.23 on the morning of September seventeenth he was already dead, and that when you opened the door you found his body lying on the floor. Would that make you change your testimony about being the one who was in the hotel at that time?"

Irene Kilby looked at him with wide, round eyes, her face showing startled surprise.

Judge Donahue leaned forward and said, "What was that? Mr. Court Reporter, read me that question. I want to get it."

The Court Reporter, in a monotone, repeated the question to Judge Donahue.

The Judge frowned, looked at the witness, then at Perry Mason, said to the witness, "Do you understand that question, Miss Kilby?"

"Yes," she said hesitantly.

"Can you answer it?"

"I . . . Yes."

"You mean that's your answer?" Mason asked.

"Yes."

"All right," Mason said. "Now, let's get at the truth of this thing. You didn't go to the hotel to call on John Callender at around two o'clock, did you?"

"No."

"But you did learn in some manner from the police, or from a source close to the police, that they had found a maid who saw Lois Fenton emerging from Callender's room at two o'clock, and you felt certain that sooner or later some witness would be found who knew that you were going to see John Callender, so you decided that you would swap identities with Lois Fenton and claim that *you* were the woman who was seen leaving his room at two o'clock in the morning, isn't that right?"

"Yes."

Mason said, "If the Court pleases, simply for the sake of
196

clearing up the record and playing fair with the witness, I will call the attention of the Court and counsel, that, according to the testimony of the witness, Faulkner, Arthur Sheldon dashed out of room 511 and entered room 510 across the corridor almost immediately after Faulkner had taken up his station in the mop closet. That was approximately 2.21 A.M. At 2.23 this witness went to John Callender's room, but if the Court will bear in mind this witness had encountered the house detective, and that the house detective had forced her to phone Callender's room, the answer immediately became obvious. Arthur Sheldon must have been in Callender's room at the time the phone rang. When Arthur Sheldon left the room, he didn't leave it in the manner that a man would leave a room where he had been visiting some person. He left it in the manner of someone who was fleeing from something. You will note that the witness, Faulkner, testified that Sheldon stepped swiftly out into the corridor, pushed the door shut behind him, jerked open the door of room 510 and vanished. It is obvious, therefore, that something must have been wrong when he left that room; that in all probability Callender was dead at that time. But it is perfectly plain that Arthur Sheldon was in that hotel room at the time the telephone rang in response to the call placed by the house detective from the room telephone in the lobby. I feel it is a fair inference that, for reasons of his own, Arthur Sheldon answered that telephone when it rang and it was Sheldon's voice the house detective heard answering the telephone, that it was to Sheldon this witness announced that she was in the lobby and was coming up.

"But so long as this witness felt it was established that John Callender had been alive at approximately 2.20, when that telephone call was placed, she didn't dare admit that she was the person who went to the room at 2.23. I think that covers the situation."

Hamilton Burger said, "Are you now claiming that Arthur Sheldon killed him?"

"*I'm* not claiming anything," Mason said, impatiently. "*I'm* trying to get the defendant in this case acquitted. As far as the murder case is concerned, you are at perfect liberty

197

to solve it. That is the end of my cross-examination of this witness.''

"And redirect examination?'' Judge Donahue asked Burger.

"None, your Honour,'' the somewhat dazed District Attorney said.

"Very well,'' Judge Donahue said. "There are some questions I want to ask this witness, but in view of the peculiar developments in this case I feel that it may not be fair to counsel for either side to ask questions in front of the jury. However, this witness has admitted giving false testimony, and I now order her into the custody of the sheriff to await such action as may be taken.''

Mason, getting to his feet, started putting papers back into his briefcase. He smiled reassuringly at his client.

"I think that does it, your Honour,'' Mason said with calm confidence. "The District Attorney can either dismiss the case against this defendant now, or we will take an adjournment until two o'clock.''

Judge Donahue took one look at Hamilton Burger's face and announced crisply, "Court will take a recess until two o'clock this afternoon.''

Chapter 22

Back in Mason's office, Paul Drake said to the lawyer, "Frankly, Perry, I don't get it."

Mason said, "The trouble with lawyers, Paul, is that they become too cynical, too sceptical."

"Lois Fenton was telling me the absolute truth. For a long while I didn't believe her. The reason I didn't believe her was because her story sounded too improbable, but it wasn't improbable. It was the most naturally logical story in the world. She told exactly what happened, and the minute I started viewing her statements in that way I knew definitely who had killed John Callender. There could only have been one person."

"Shoot," Drake said.

Mason said, "I ran on to Harry Cogswell in the corridor. Therefore, I knew he had called on Callender at about 1.20. Lois Fenton said she left Callender at two o'clock. A maid saw her in the corridor, and saw Callender standing in the doorway.

"When Arthur Sheldon left Callender's room, he acted very much as though he were escaping from something. When Arthur Sheldon checked out of the hotel he put a DO NOT DISTURB sign on Callender's door. He must, therefore, have known at the time Callender was murdered and he wanted to keep the crime from being discovered as long as possible. That was only natural. Under the circumstances and having occupied the room across the hall, he needed time to clear his own skirts."

"You mean Sheldon committed the crime?"

"I mean that if Sheldon knew he was dead when he put tnat DO NOT DISTURB sign on the door, he must have known he was dead when he left Callender's room because

199

the evidence shows that no one communicated with Sheldon after that. There were no phone calls to his room, no one called on him.''

Drake slowly nodded.

"Therefore, it is obvious that Sheldon must have been the one who answered the telephone when the house detective called Callender's room. Evidently Sheldon thought that it might be Lois Fenton calling, because he knew Callender wanted to see her, so he decided to answer the phone and warn her against calling up. When he heard the voice of a strange woman he simply posed as Callender. Remember he had no need to say very much other than 'hello.' The woman did the talking. She said she was in the lobby, that the house detective had made her call, that she was coming up. Sheldon simply hung up the phone, dashed back across the hall to his own room, and waited for an alarm to be given. He was probably sick with fright right then.''

"Go ahead," Drake said.

"That's all there is to it," Mason said. "When no alarm was given, Sheldon knew he stood a chance. He waited for the coast to clear and then checked out. He then had the satisfaction of knowing some woman had called on Callender and had failed to give the alarm. So he put his DO NOT DISTURB sign on Callender's door as he went out. That should have delayed discovery of the crime sufficiently to have given Sheldon a chance to confuse the issues. But Callender had left instructions that at a certain time he was to be aroused by having coffee brought to his room. He had a habit of requiring coffee as soon as he awakened.''

Drake said, "That's nice reasoning, Perry, but exactly what did happen, and how did it happen?''

Mason said, "I knew that Cogswell had called on Callender. He had made a hurried trip from Palomino just as soon as I had given him and Irene Kilby the fans. Therefore, it was logical to suppose that Cogswell and Irene made a rush trip down from Palomino to give those fans to Callender. The doctor's theory was quite correct. Callender was holding up that fan in front of him when his assailant, using the Japanese sword as a weapon and his actions being screened by the fact that Callender was holding the open fan in front of him, simply plunged the blade into Callender's chest, stabbing right through the fan.''

Drake nodded.

''Now why had Callender opened the fan? Undoubtedly to show it to someone. Why did he want to show it to someone? Because he wanted to prove something in connection with the fan or in connection with the ownership of the fan.

''Lois Fenton told me that Sheldon had previously rented a room down in the rooming house on Lagmore Street because she wanted a room for Jasper Fenton. Jasper was to go there.

''You can see what happened. Jasper Fenton went to the hotel. He kept his two o'clock appointment with John Callender, and John Callender told him very cold-bloodedly that Jasper could tell his sister that unless she returned to him Jasper Fenton was going to jail. He had just received one of the fans from Cogswell. He held that fan up to show Jasper that I hadn't found the horse, only a fan. That was Jasper Fenton's opportunity.

''Jasper Fenton knew that Lois wouldn't go back to Callender no matter what happened. That meant Callender was going to send Fenton to jail. The plumes of the fan momentarily screened Fenton from Callender's eyes. The Japanese sword was on the table. The first Callender knew, the blade was being shoved into his chest. He dropped the fan and grabbed at the blade, cutting his fingers to the bone. He died almost instantly.''

''But why did Jasper Fenton go back to the room at 2.44?'' Drake asked.

Mason said, ''That was the only decent thing Jasper Fenton ever did. After he had left the hotel, he remembered that the fan was lying there in a pool of blood. He knew it was his sister's fan. He knew that the fan would link her with the crime. He went back to the hotel, went up to Callender's room, went in, grabbed the fan, slapped it against the wall to remove the blood, concealed it under his coat and came out.

''Notice the evidence, Paul. The man was wearing an

201

overcoat when he came to the hotel. He pushed open the door of Callender's room and went in without knocking. Why? Because he knew that a knock would do no good. He also knew that the door was unlocked. If he hadn't known Callender was dead, he would have knocked on the door."

Drake nodded.

"Fenton got the fan," Mason said, "He went to the room in the rooming house—the one Arthur Sheldon had taken for him. There he became panic stricken. He had this blood-soaked fan and he didn't know what to do with it. He went out to get a drink. He kept on drinking. In the meantime, Sheldon had checked out of the Richmell Hotel. He had no place to go. He remembered this room that he had secured for Jasper Fenton. He decided he'd go up and share the room with Fenton. He found the key on the board. He entered the room. He found the blood-soaked fan. He called Lois. Lois thought Sheldon had killed Callender, and Sheldon, making a martyr of himself to save Lois, because he thought she was guilty, decided to skip out so the police would blame the crime on him. And that is the situation in a nutshell, Paul. I'd have had the case solved a long time ago if I'd only believed my client was telling me the truth when she told me that wildly improbable story about the fan."

"What'll they do with Fenton?" Drake asked.

Mason grinned. "That's Burger's headache. Callender was blackmailing Fenton. He was forcing himself on Fenton's sister. No jury in the world will give him first-degree murder. It he gets a good lawyer he can make it manslaughter."

"But what was Irene Kilby doing in that room for the ten minutes she was there?"

"Searching for that agreement. When she found Callender dead she was just cold-blooded enough and just selfish enough to look around and try and find that agreement. She looked every place except the place where it was."

"Where's that?"

Mason grinned. "I don't know for certain, Paul, but let's look at the evidence. Callender kept that room in the hotel. He came up from the Valley, trying to get away from the heat, and he carried that Japanese sword with him. The reason he carried that Japanese sword with him was because the handle of that sword was the place he'd chosen to conceal the documents he was using, the agreement Lois had signed, the forged cheques."

"My God, Perry, that sounds logical."

"It is logical," Mason said. "That's where the documents were."

"How do you know?"

Mason smiled. "The sword was in court as an exhibit. After court adjourned and during the excitement I pulled out the pin and slipped the handle off the blade. The documents were inside."

Mason opened his billfold, took out the agreement signed by Irene Kilby and Lois Fenton, said with a grin, "After all, a lawyer should do *something* for a client. I left the forged cheques in there for Hamilton Burger to discover."

About the Author

Erle Stanley Gardner is the king of American mystery fiction. A criminal lawyer, he filled his mystery masterpieces with intricate, fascinating, ever-twisting plots. Challenging, clever, and full of surprises, these are whodunits in the best tradition. During his lifetime, Erle Stanley Gardner wrote 146 books, 85 of which feature Perry Mason.